The Snow Violin

The Snow Violin

Michel Louyot

translated from the French by
Catherine Cauvin-Higgins

LEAKY BOOT PRESS

The Snow Violin
by Michel Louyot
Translated from the French by
Catherine Cauvin-Higgins

First published in the English language in 2014 by
Leaky Boot Press
http://www.leakyboot.com

ISBN: 978-1-909849-10-5

To Paul and Volodia
in the blue Lada

Shadow in its deepest meaning is the invisible saurian's tail that man still drags behind him. Neatly separated, it becomes the sacred snake of mystery. Only apes are using theirs to show off.

C. G. Jung, *Life and the Soul*

Prologue

On a mid-August afternoon in Paris in the nineteen seventies, P, a person of huge stature, carrying a small red suitcase, is about to go down the stairs leading to the subway at the Latour-Maubourg station. For over half an hour now I have been thinking of him with the hope of meeting him, while knowing perfectly well that he is not supposed to be in the capital currently, because he is spending his vacations in the mountains. From the terrace of the café where I am sitting, I observe him without him seeing me and, instead of getting up and running to call out to him, I gather my thoughts, collect myself and focus in his direction. P stops on the third or fourth step, hesitates, turns around, goes back up the stairs, as if he had forgotten something, looks in my direction, and sees me. It has been almost a year since he last came to this part of town. Did he pretend to believe that I was the one who made him come this way, while, in fact, it was his psychic power that drew me to the rendezvous location he had chosen?

I met the man with the small red suitcase in Meudon, at the Saint-Georges boarding school. We were perfecting our Russian language skills. The Saint-Georges Orthodox community had settled in a pink villa opening onto a vast park, shaded by an ancient cedar tree. The linguistic summer camp brought together lively Italians, Brits faithfully sticking to dishwashing duties, liberated young German women, a Japanese man who played Bach on his violin and was writing an essay about Dostoyevsky's influence on the Meiji period novel. How were the friars who were running Saint-Georges able to create a true, albeit temporary, family out of this eclectic bunch? Undoubtedly, "uncle" Kolya and "aunt" Nadya had a flair for bringing together, around the campfire, Russophiles and anti-Soviets, spies and spy hunters, pirozhki, and verbs of motion. They were helped in this ardent endeavor by several engaging young women like Svetlana, Lidya and Ira; the latter wrote me disenchanted witty letters on lavender or gray paper, the tint depending on the degree of her disenchantment.

"I want to break away from my current life style, quit drinking whiskey, quit drinking vodka, quit drinking, stop thinking, stop crying. I want to live. It seems to me that you are intelligent, although I do not know what that means, maybe the ability not to do foolish things. I anticipate what you can do and what you won't do. Come visit, rent a tuxedo, and I'll buy a silver pendant at the flea market. I received my work permit papers, but I don't have work. Last year, it was the other way around. I am in Evian, it rains like it does in Petersburg, everything is fine. Life goes on, I lunch, I dine, I talk, I read, I write letters… How depressing! Did you read 'Look at the Harlequins!'? I'd like to read your poems. Yesterday, P came with his wife and their many children in a small yellow van. Now, it is autumn in Meudon, and the leaves fall in the park making an incomprehensible sound." Ira's letters, all tinged with the sorrow of exile, slid like glass beads on the invisible thread of time, about to put an end to this impossible romance. "An agent cannot allow himself the slightest lapse while on post: only well-earned, possibly romantic, rest is admissible between two missions." With his craggy profile, an uncommon height and build, P knew how to make use of his rugged looks. I saw him throw a dagger twenty meters, driving it straight into the trunk of a tree in the park, without batting an eyelid. In reality, the man was much more complex than his appearance would lead one to believe. His minuscule handwriting revealed a taste for secrecy as well as a penetrating mind, an asset in his investigative work. An uncanny charm emanated from the sharp contrasts in the multifaceted sides of his persona. P used this peculiarity with success when approaching people, whether for agent recruiting or turn-around. Did he know instantly when he had won the game? He'd taken his time, though. "A long, painstaking job." He excelled at collecting minute data, confronting measured and verified information, and then putting it into perspective. The Americans had tried to arrive before P. A fake cab carted me about at two hundred kilometers per hour through Paris streets, deserted at this time of year. I did not lose my cool, but turned down the offer. I remained a Frenchman for better "and mostly for worse," P added, harboring no illusions about the march of History or the fickleness of nations. "Pétain supporters in winter, Gaullists in summer." His cheeky tone, however, and his skepticism bordering on cynicism, hid convictions that were all the stronger because never expressed. "If the secret agent has something in common with the mystic, it is his belief in the devil." Conversations thus lasted deep into the night under the Meudon cedar tree or under the chestnut trees on Place Stalingrad, as we stared, with irony and without flinching, at the beer bubbles bursting at the surface in our glasses. P did not know yet that on May 1, 1981, under the name "Paul," he would meet Vladimir Ippolitovich Vetrov in the small Moscow park located behind the Borodino Museum.

Get ready Vetrov! The rattling noise of opening and closing gates, grinding of keys in the locks, and the warder clearing his throat before spitting on the floor, his face indistinct in the wan half-light. Which god or devil put a curse on this Russia that has been, is, and will remain for a long time to come, an immense prison? There is no spite in the warder's rasping voice. I can only perceive his silhouette; he dares not look at me. Does he know the charges against me? Does he wonder if one day he will be the one called at the crack of dawn by another warder? Those are Russia's usual ways! This must be why the order was whispered, barely audible, by this spineless character. He is, however, not entirely inhuman, a guy similar to millions of others encountered on trains, going both ways, at the camp. What distinguishes warders from inmates, political prisoners from petty criminals? Maybe this is what makes us different from the Nazis. In Russia everything is vague and ill-defined, nobody knows who does what, roles are interchangeable, everyone spends their life talking and acting contrary to what they think; why would I have been an exception? How impudent of me to have believed I could distinguish myself, emerge from the mass, be part of the elite, leave the country, play my own score. And what a disillusion! Inexorable, the fate that had once and for all cursed the Russians brings me back to the common condition; get ready Vetrov, the moment of truth has come!

Take your time! Does he want to prolong the agony, did he come early to find out more about what goes on in the head of a man in such moments? Reading Vetrov's last thoughts is worth the trip! There are loads of people just about anywhere in the world who, if they had been informed of the event, would give anything to be in his shoes! Could it be that he received special instructions on how to lead this last conversation? What if I deliver an ultimate and sensational revelation? Nothing must be neglected. A moment of weakness, and even the toughest end up coming clean. A last little secret, Vetrov, and here is the warder appointed director of the prison! Our Soviet homeland has always been generous towards informers. Take your time, Vetrov. Take all of the time they condescend to grant you. This time belongs to you, don't squander it. The jail cell is the ideal place for a final confrontation; neglect nothing, scour every recess in your mind, open the floodgates of memory!

A storm of old and recent memories going round and round, swelling up, jumbling together. The warder's instruction set rolling a process of recollection with a keenness unknown to me up to now. This is the last show I have the opportunity to see, as the spectator, the actor and the director. Will I get, at last, the answer to the questions that have been haunting me for so long? *Who are you deep down, Vetrov?* The warder sat on a stool in the corridor. He keeps mumbling some gibberish, as if he had a hangover. Which part does he pretend to play? Is he the prompter? And his masters, who were mine, are they so naive as to believe they are the authors of the unfolding play? Still avoiding looking at me, he lights up a cigarette after half-making the gesture of offering me one. Is it the first time he was asked to do this dirty job? Now is not the time to pity him. He has always obeyed the orders. He is merely a tiny cog in this huge machine grinding up the human beings in this vast country. A fifth of the earth's landmass, and tentacles sprawling all over, the red octopus thought it could seize the world. It was animated by a formidable energy, a strength born of despair, frustration, desire for revenge. For a long time it cashed in on the feeling of injustice among the hungry, the exploited and the wretched of the earth. *You think too much, Vetrov.* And you would not be where you are, had you been able to draw a veil over, put a stop to inconvenient questioning. You weren't the only one to doubt. You could have gone on as though nothing ever happened. Didn't you live your adult life during the "stagnation" period? It is not difficult to stagnate. All one has to do is to wait for things to pass. Most of your colleagues were as lucid as you, but they did not try to stand out. The secret agent must melt into the crowd, Vetrov, you broke the basic rules. You no longer wanted to hug the walls or pull a long face. How foolish it was on your part to believe you could act according to your thoughts! You should have grinned, and borne it, as the others did. How many of your colleagues hid themselves away for entire weekends in their dachas, behind drawn curtains, stuffing themselves with caviar paid for in foreign currencies, drinking vodka straight from the bottle and singing Dark Eyes, Okudzhava's and Vysotsky's songs or the Beatles! You forgot where you came from, Vetrov! You failed the fundamental values of the workers' country; a mad dog is what you are. Don't be surprised if they put your fate in the veterinarian's hands. *A mad dog.* I hardly heard the clicking of the key in the lock. The newcomer, a woman, looks daggers at me and insults me. It's not the veterinarian yet, but it is already about cleaning up the place. The comrade sluices down the corridor, then my cell, by the pailful. Scratchy noise of the scrubbing brush on the slab. Little Soviet music that I prefer over any patriotic tune. How could I forget the grayness, the decay, the insidious fear gnawing at humans! I belong to this country, I don't disown it, but I refuse to close my eyes, *matushka*, Mother Russia! Everything is falling apart, the fabric is fraying all over, the ship is taking in water. Open your eyes, *matushka*!

Your friends did not forget you, Vetrov. As if afraid of being heard by the comrade, the warder vacantly whispers a few words. What game is he playing? Which friends is he talking about? Does he truly think that I'm going to rush headlong into this ridiculous trap? He may be acting in good faith, unaware of the stratagem in which he was asked to take part. Unless he is smarter than he appears to be, nowadays, he would not be the only one with several irons in the fire. The ship is rolling from one side to the other, the proponents of a less versus more open society are fighting for power. Who is right today will be wrong tomorrow. Whoever doesn't have the presence of mind to jump off the train heading in the wrong direction will be in trouble! *Your friends did not forget you, Vetrov.* Could he be right? But how to find out since it is forbidden to speak to him? No need to take risks as long as the vixen is still going about her business in the corridor! Assuming my friends did not forget me, isn't the best proof of my loyalty to go all the way, not turning away from it, to live in the here and now the last hours of my life?

Soon after the shrew has closed the door, the roach reappears. Not only do I no longer feel like squashing this creature who has been crawling around my cell since the day I arrived, but I am now accustomed to the nocturnal insect with its flat body, chewing on dry bread chunks and grazing my blanket. I could even feel sympathy for this light-fleeing insect. *You're just a cockroach, Vetrov, an ordinary cockroach*, relentlessly repeated one of the investigating officers. What if the insult was a compliment? And what if my ultimate companion, my last link with the world, was showing me the way? I, too, decided to flee the surreal light, to forget everything we were force-fed. I no longer accept declaring that white is black, that lies are truth; once we've opened our eyes, we can't close them again. No matter how hard you tried for the last seventy-years to clean, purge, liquidate, eliminate, eradicate, weeds grow back between the stones. *From childhood through old age, Soviet citizens are surrounded by the State's solicitude.* The more you trumpet your slogans, the more the country falls into decay, poorly assembled window frames letting the cold seep in. *For the first time in History, the prosperity, the economic and social well-being of all the people are the priority of the government*; erased street names, eluded topics of conversation, courtyards cluttered with rubbish; *for over sixty-years, the Soviets have lived with no exploiters and no exploited*; circumlocution of the mind, wobbling manhole covers, gossip, rumors and insinuations; *nowhere else in the world do people smile so well and so sincerely as in the Soviet Union*, rubble littering the ground, rundown buildings, a guy standing watch in the entrance, balconies crowded with foodstuffs and furniture, puffing tramways, potholes filled with rotten water, stench of sour cabbage in the staircase, *everything for mankind, everything for the good of humanity*, phone calls in the middle of the night, cigarette butts scattered under a bench, rawboned dogs, rusty awning, perfidious innuendos, car on blocks, ivy overgrowing everything, indefinable fear blanketing everything, *cordiality, genuine collectivism characterize the Soviet people*, sallow face, sticky eyes, purulent open wound of memory, with its cracks and potholes pervading me, when I thought I could suppress it, getting back at me, working its way through the slippery paved lanes, and following the glum corridors of nightmare; *everything for mankind, everything for the good of humanity*; one cannot escape after experiencing the wan light of dawn and evasive glances.

The cockroach no longer fears me. It curls up in my blanket, snuggles up to me, slips between my toes, travels along my leg, stops, one of its antennae twitching; is this its way to show me affection or to relay a message from the kingdom below? Subterranean Russia, Muscovite undergrounds, hubbub, raucous shouting of men, shrill cries of women, smells of sweat, cabbage, cheap perfumes, poorly refined gasoline, brine, mildew, musty smells; little cockroach, this is the world you represent and are reminding me of, a murky Russia, a decaying country, rushing back to my memory; patched up buses, grayish housing blocks, exhausted locomotives, puny trees, threadbare armchairs, haggard looks, pictures of those who did not return, head shaking, eloquent silences, endless winters, useless cranes imploring the sky, another Russia, *there is only one Russia, and it is Soviet*, a simple Russia without falsification, howling in suffering, screaming its naked truth, nightmarish and dreary, I prefer it over your Potemkin's villages and your fallacious phantasmagoria; *you're spitting on the hand that gave you everything, Vetrov*, I'm spitting on nobody, I just see things the way they are and I say so; *you're insulting your homeland*, I am sympathizing with it in its suffering, I am rebelling against those who took it upon themselves to turn the dream into a nightmare. Can't you see the degree of depravity in utopias? *If you're so disgusted by Russia, Vetrov, why did you come back?*

Malicious pleasure, a voyeur's morbid desire? No, I did not come back to revel in watching my country fall. *Your country needs you no more, Vetrov, in a few hours you'll be just a carcass the neighborhood dogs will share out.*

Bullet holes in my skin, rushing blood, exploded skull. I thought I prepared myself for the last scene; like the poet smiling at the firing squad, I imagined myself defying my murderers, I thought I had become indifferent to death, I had forgotten everything that was, is, linking me to life, *the cockroach, Vetrov, what will happen to it without you*, yes, the cockroach, and all this Moscow gloom, *dirty snow*, those childhood smells, *sour cabbage*, walks through parks, in forests, *the spring breeze through the tender green leaves of the birch trees*, strong tastes, *dry fish from the Caspian sea* and the first shot of vodka, *it's up to you not to sever the bonds*, but do I still have a choice, *your friends did not forget you, Vetrov*, do I still have friends here or over there caring about a pariah, a condemned man? *Here or there, Vetrov, the time has come to decide,* I am unable to detest my jailer, we are carved out of the same wood, there is this familiar thing in the way he treats me, specific to our people, that I missed abroad, and yet I cannot trust him, *double-faced Russia*, does he read my soul? *One foot inside, one foot outside*, country of wanderers, would he be ready to clear off with me? *There is no way you'd become a petty bourgeois, Vetrov*, could he have a plan? It would be foolish, how to escape from this bunker? Even if by chance we succeeded in getting out, where to flee and how?

The black creature found refuge in the pocket of my prisoner jacket. With its legs folded under its body, it seems to be dozing off. No better time to review one's life. *Stirring up memories is dangerous, Vetrov.* Holding them back is even worse. They're moaning and groaning, feeling this is their last chance to be heard. So here they are, hurrying back with a vengeance! If at least the happy images could prevail, but no, it's the others, humiliations, grudges, failures, lost opportunities that insist on occupying the place; they become embedded like cysts, provoking me, scoffing at me. Is there no other choice for me than watching, powerless, my ghosts whirling around in my head? A storm at sea is nothing in comparison with what I'm going through; a true upheaval that makes me sick. *You asked for it, Vetrov.* This time, the hag did not glance at me. She shoots her arrow sidewise while walking by the spyhole, I can hear her rinse the floor, wring out the mop, and the scrubbing brush scratching, scratching as she moves away, to the warder's relief, now able to get back to his post and sit on his chair. Could he be under suspicion? Yes, I did ask for it, the old hag is right, I asked for it because I could not stand it anymore, turning like a hypnotized moth around a lamp no longer lighting anything. *You are your worst enemy, Vetrov!* You could have remained the one you were, the son of Ippolit Vasilevich, mobilized in 1941, who survived the war, and the son of Maria Danilovna, the maid. *If they were still alive and could see what you became, your parents would be overwhelmed with shame. Think of the victorious soldier, Vetrov;* I did not forget about him, and I did not forget my mother's hearty smile. *Here is your last chance to redeem yourself in their eyes, remember the person you were once.* A child of the people, living simply in the communal apartment on Kirov Street. *You didn't complain, Vetrov, that you had to share the kitchen, the bathroom, the shower with other occupants of the building.* And it didn't prevent me from studying relentlessly, from spending every evening reading. *At that time, you didn't have absurd pretensions.* I believed in opportunities, I believed in the advent of Communism. *You owe your social advancement to the Soviet people, Vetrov.* I will have seen it all, from inside and from a ringside seat, the Cold War, the Thaw, and Détente, expansion and decline. *The Party gave you everything, Comrade.* An entire life inextricably intertwined with my country's life. I disown nothing; how could I dismiss happy memories, my teenage years in Moscow, the warm camaraderie at the canteen, storming the girls' dorms, chess games in the parks, campfires in the wintry forest, padded jackets, felt boots, the cracking of larch twigs, and all those nights spent counting shooting stars. *You believed in a radiant future, Vetrov, you were running toward the future as fast as your legs could carry you. Vladimir Ippolitovich Vetrov, three medals, three times crowned junior league champion of the Soviet Union in 100, 200 and 400 meter races*; yes, I was this young man, why would I say otherwise, I no longer need to protect myself, fill the cracks, I have nothing to lose anymore.

You have everything to lose, Vetrov, in a few hours, can you hear bullets hissing by, can you see your body collapsing in slush, if not in mud—the weather changes fast these days; what do I care about the weather, what do I care about the end of the story, since I have accomplished my duty; *everyone makes mistakes, Vetrov, it is up to you to spare those who love you tears and grief;* as if I still had a chance to rebound, the time has come, I've always known I would end my life in jail, I've always felt I could not escape my fate, yet I spent most of my time beside myself or outside of myself. I thought I could become a new man, I was led astray by illusory promises, like millions of others I lost sight of myself, all that was left of me was an empty shell, a mask, I had become an apparatchik, a member, an underling, a dead leaf caught in the wind of History. *The wind blows wherever it wants, Vetrov, you know that.* By dint of stating my name, Comrade, I forgot its meaning. Vetrov, from *veter*, the wind. I am not the wind, but I know I proceed from it, like each of us. Yes, the wind blows freely; it's only over time that I started listening to its rustling. I am no longer the dead leaf fluttering around, unaware of the force moving it.

You're going astray, Vetrov, you let yourself be diverted from your duty. So many times over the course of the trial you called me a deviationist, an opportunist. *The Party alone knows what is just and good for the masses.* I became capable of independent thinking, *you thought you could substitute yourself for the ruling vanguard*, I believed I could act independently, go on ahead, *you doubted the People's ability to open new perspectives*, I forgot the lessons repeated over and over during childhood, teenage and my militant years, *enlightenment can only come from the Party*; the Soviet people demonstrated its ability to change the course of rivers. *Pravda, Vetrov, for a long time truth inspired your behavior.* There was no limit then to what I could hope as a young pioneer! *"Lenin's forehead" was the nickname your mother gave you.* How proud she was of her little Volodia, Maria Danilovna! *There was no limit to what you could hope, Vetrov.* The communist dream was shaping up, *electrification plus the soviets*, it was the time of sputniks, astronauts, Baikonur, triumphant Soviet science, *détente facilitated expansion*, Moscow positioned itself to the south and the west, China was on our side. My wishes were fulfilled when I was accepted to the Bauman Technical Institute. A brilliant career in engineering was awaiting me. *You didn't know your place, Vetrov.* I kept believing in this "radiant future" I was cheerfully running toward. *You were going like the wind to meet your destiny*; you don't know how right you are! If I had not been running so fast, the Dynamo Club would never have noticed me nor sent me to training in Abkhazia, I would not have met the cute little blonde, *Svetlana is the cause of nothing in your downfall*, I know, my sunshine, it's not your fault, life goes on, it will soon be springtime, *it's up to you to figure out and decide whether you want to hear the birds chirping outside your window in the morning one more time*, it's for me to go through this self-inflicted ordeal; *remember stolen kisses on public benches*, our walks in Moscow parks, the light touch of our hands, how could I forget the suffering I caused, the blows dealt by me, the blood gushing from open wounds, I have sinned through my fault, through my most grievous fault, I am guilty before God and mankind.

What a downhill, Vetrov, the Soviet had given you a chance, a unique chance, the opportunity to practice another sport, a much more ambitious one, *the Big Game, in the service of the workers' homeland*, it's the Dynamo Club which led me straight to the State Committee for Security, *through the "School in the Woods," the Higher School of Intelligence*, I would get the opportunity to discover the world and work in the field, in the vanguard, for the benefit of my country.

The cockroach is now nestling in the hollow of my hand. It wiggles under the stroking of my fingertips. The warder, who half opened the spyhole, acts as if he doesn't notice the scene. *You got a parcel, Vetrov.* A white shirt and the burgundy tie Svetlana gave me as a present soon after we arrived in Paris. *Remember springtime, Vetrov, Svetlana's springy footsteps in the bedroom in the morning, the fluttering of the birds' wings at the window.*

Why are prisons always so dank? Why are the cell walls always grayish? Why is the light coming down from the small window always so pale? How many poor fellows have rotted in this dump before me? And how much more time am I going to languish here? I went through several months of questioning, the investigating officers took turns relentlessly, getting enough from me to write seven thick volumes. I went along with their game, I answered willingly, opposing no resistance whatsoever to their countless questions. Then the sentence was read half-heartedly by a magistrate presiding over an ad hoc court. Why did they defer the execution several times? Here I am, beginning to hope again. *The Russian dream.* I am shrouded in a pearly light. *It's snowing.* I look up and see the flakes dancing. Some fly closer to others, merge into one another; others on the contrary flee, disperse and fly away forever. In growing numbers, they land and die on the dirty window pane. Light farewell kisses, my country isn't a country, it's winter, it's the snow from the beginning of my life, first snow, white cocoon of childhood, heart-uplifting snow, rumor-muffling snow, lullaby to the ear, caress on the tip of the nose, snow crunching and cracking under footsteps, melting snow, cheerful snow, gloomy snow, gray, mildewed snow, last snow. The snow falls thicker, snowflakes are swarming against the window, missing nothing of what goes on in the prisoner's heart. *It's not going to be for today either; they had a wild time all night long.* Where is the old woman coming from? Lost in my thoughts, I didn't hear any jingling. The minute her madam face appeared I could smell her fetid breath as she angrily slammed the spyhole shut. The cockroach's elytra shine like a clip on the dry-blood color tie.

Remember the white shirt, Vetrov, white like snow, white like the violin born from the swarm of snowflakes gently dancing in the wind. In which childhood did I hear the story of this violin showing me the way? Did grandmother tell it to me? Was it a Russian tale, a Tartar or a Gypsy tale? Or did I dream it, invent it? *This would not be your first invention, Vetrov.* The dividing line between dream and reality is fuzzier and fuzzier. And I have more and more difficulty distinguishing day from night. I can sleep during the day and stay awake until dawn. I must have dozed off for a couple of hours or so, unaware of it. My life is paced by the cockroach's life rhythm; it shakes itself, slides on the blanket and crawls on the wall to go hide in a crack. It is now snowing intermittently. A treacherous fog surrounds the prison yard, choking it. I am dragging myself about my tiny space which I have paced around thousands of times, turning over the same thoughts, beset and torn apart by the same questions. Should I assume the fate I chose to the death? But to what extent did I decide my fate? Has fate taken its revenge by making me commit an odious crime? Shouldn't I risk my all to go on living, make amends and take care of those who are hoping for my return? *Think about the white shirt, Vetrov, snow-white like the violin.* My grandmother from Simbirsk used to say "The tragedy of mankind is and has been to believe that one can grab the snow violin." For a long time I myself wanted to believe in its existence. With millions of others I went in the pursuit of the violin, but grandmother was right, I've learned this at my expense, the tragedy of the Russian people and of those they enslaved is rooted in their attempt to capture the magic of this elusive instrument.

When I joined the Service, I had hoped to contribute to the country's development and modernization. *And that's what you did, Vetrov, until you drifted into delusion.* I remember it all, the long hours studying, the training sessions in the field; how to recruit an agent, how to outwit tailing, how to take delivery from a dead letter box, how to resist capitalist propaganda. I learned all this in the bright classrooms of the school nestled among pines and birches. I have been initiated by our best experts into the techniques of scientific intelligence, into geopolitics, Western foreign languages, *and you became one of* the most brilliant elements of the famous Directorate T in charge of scientific and technical espionage. I did not place a foot wrong, I blindly believed that the Dzerzhinsky School's engineers of human soul were masters of their craft, I did not doubt, I did not know then that Russia was sick.

You knew it, Vetrov, there is another Vetrov in you who knew. I sensed something while I was singing the International at the top of my voice, but I didn't want to know despite the spate of revelations during the Twentieth Congress. Khrushchev was not an angel but he had understood that the time had come to make concessions. *Take him as a model, Vetrov.* A formidable self-criticism after which the country could rebound, make a clean start, start from scratch again. But who gave him the right, who allowed us to erase thirty years of Stalinism, to forget the black cars patrolling city streets at night, the men in leather coats who knocked at people's doors? They were not surprised to see that they were expected, everyone had dried their tears before "they" arrived, the guilty, *the enemies of the people*, gave themselves up without rebelling, there was an implacable silence in staircases, behind the doors, everyone was holding their breath, listening anxiously. What if my turn had come? I did not want to know; to me, the Soviet Union was Stalingrad, the Great Patriotic War, victory over fascism, and soon victory over capitalism. I had a bright future ahead of me; *you specialized in electronic devices for missiles*, at age thirty-three I was offered a job at the Ministry of Foreign Trade, *which was your cover*, and I was proud to move into an apartment on Kutuzov Avenue with my loving Svetlana who bought a splendid Chinese rug with blue roses to celebrate the event.

You were walking on a carpet of roses, Vetrov, and it was just the start of a destiny placed under the sign of success. *You lived a fairy tale*; life was as beautiful as in grandmother's stories, I strutted about like the Cat of Kazan, I hunted the whale in the White Sea, I flew away on the back of the bird of paradise. *Grandmother had warned you, though*; the image box was full of stories that ended poorly: the soldier who wants to go to paradise but is sent to hell, a *muzhik* caged by his parrot, the warrior Anika who thinks he can defeat death, the last days of the jester Farnos The Red Nose. *Reaching happiness is not enough, Vetrov, one has to be able to preserve it*, that's what I haven't been able to do; *if you had been the only one affected by the consequences of your insane actions, but others, innocent people, have to pick up the pieces, like Vladik, your son;* my sweet child who started walking on the rug with the blue roses, *Vladik who now doesn't get a wink of sleep at night and is moving heaven and earth to save his father,* I failed to protect my loved ones' happiness, *because of the other Vetrov,* the one I repressed, *the shadow of Vetrov,* which I refused to see; *you're a cockroach, Vetrov, a pitiful informer, you no longer deserve to see the light of day, you no longer deserve to see the red star shining over our Soviet homeland.*

I envy the cockroach. What does it care about the red star that they all pretend to revere when from top to bottom there is nobody left to believe in its meaning. What does it care if life is permeated by lies and the empire of the spooks is ruled by cant and black market. Could it be more free than all of us? It comes and goes as it pleases. It's up to it to leave the cell by slipping through the poorly jointed window frame, crossing the courtyard to hide in the kitchen or in the jail director's office. It prefers to share my fate. If granted the favor to express my last wish, I'd ask for my little cellmate to stay with me until my last breath. Little cockroach, you are the embodiment of this invisible and intangible shadow to which I did not want to pay attention, and which slowly imposed itself upon me and turned my life upside down.

Your life is hanging by a thread, Vetrov, little Vladik, my sunshine, will I keep my dignity when they grab me? Will I be strong enough to stay standing with a smile on my face, like the poet? *They thought about everything, Vetrov, they know, they're experienced; first, they'll tie your hands behind your back,* why bother, *they'll hold you till the end, they'll place a chair behind you in case you collapse,* to die sitting or sprawling, never! *That's what they all say but that is to ignore the fright, the panic which takes over the convict when the last minute draws near;* I am already on the other side, *that's what you think now, remember your childhood and the wild flowers on the banks of the Volga River, think about the white shirt,* I can already see it spattered with the red roses of my blood, *don't expect to put on a show,* the judges didn't have the courage to look me in the eyes when they gave their verdict, *you'd better be ready for an execution on the sly, Vetrov,* with no funeral, no grave, *and no pension for Svetlana,* sweetheart, my sunshine, my blue rose, *a Russian woman with a heart immense like this country,* she wants me to look presentable as I face death, *remember the first light of dawn, wind chasing the clouds away, birches' tender greens,* happiness that was and which I could not keep because of the other Vetrov, the one I didn't want to see or hear, *Vetrov's shadow,* can one live without a shadow?

Whatever you say, whatever you do, the shadow always wins. It pretends to knuckle under, faithful dog attached to its master, but as soon as the master tries to grab it, it slips away, does as it likes, plays hide-and-seek, prances about, fools around; yes, it is the truly crazy side of the human mind, taking you to places you wouldn't have ventured to on your own. It can't stay in one place, you think it's behind you, but it's before you, showing the way, staying off the beaten track, it adores shortcuts, *it got you lost, Vetrov, although they had warned you at the School in the woods,* yes... I could have kept walking on the rug with the blue roses and climbing the rungs of the hierarchical ladder, *you became uncontrollable,* I was no longer willing to be the one you wanted me to be; *you ended up looking like the portrait our enemies drew of you to better deceive you.* It's true that at maturity, at the height of my career, I threw overboard all the lessons learned during my training years. This whole undertaking, aiming at depersonalizing me without my knowing, turned out to have been in vain. *You cut yourself off the living body of the Soviet Union,* I doggedly wanted to become somebody, a human being with his light and dark sides. *You made the mistake of being right too soon, Vetrov.*

But before being wrong, in your eyes, wasn't I an effective agent? *You got it quicker than the others, your made excellent grades, you seemed equally gifted for analysis and action.* Analysis and action. That was precisely the way they labeled the end-of-curriculum internship which was about the oldest human emotion: fear. "Who has never been scared?" had asked the officer in charge of getting agents ready before they were sent abroad on assignment. Of course, nobody answered. The expert's lips were extremely thin. He first saw service under Beria, starting his career. A trembling hand, a twitching lid, a cheek turning pale or blushing, a shiver, a jump, the expert in psychic mechanisms knew every single symptom of fear. The internship was tailored for intelligence officers whose duties required some finesse. For its part, the action service operated, if need be, before in order to weaken the prey or after to finish it off. "You are artists," he used to say with a thin voice. It's up to you to sense what is the most effective method. A terrorized correspondent will not do good work. Proceed with the utmost care! Unnerving, disconcerting, alarming, threatening. Dosage is everything, and such means are applicable only to especially tough game situations. With others, it is preferable to proceed by hints or suggestions in order to make the recalcitrant eventually eat out of your hand. Men are big children. Don't hesitate to play the part of the big brother, the confidant, if not the confessor. One of these days, even the most close-mouthed will feel the need to confide to an attentive ear in order to end the solitude which frightens human beings as much as the ancient fear of the dark.

Working in the background as a spook, I was an expert in intelligence, successful at extorting information by stroking the keys of psychological mechanisms, I was that man; *you could have remained this man, you could become this man again. It's up to you.* How could I accept the idea of becoming subservient again when, under the blue cedar tree, I distanced myself from the old me, the Soviet "new" man? *You let yourself be bewitched by the flames that will end up setting you ablaze.* I saw the jester Farnos The Red Nose being burnt, *you think you can thumb your nose at death, it will have the last word,* there is no escape from it, *the ultimate skill is to delay the fatal outcome,* however much you try, you won't be able to assassinate the wind, the clouds, the snow, *we have plenty of time, time belongs to us*, the cat of Kazan himself could not catch all the mice on the planet, *we built impassable walls*, you attempted to destroy the tradition, it will rise from its ashes, *the future is the reflection of who we are*, the Russians themselves won't be fooled much longer by your cock-and-bull-stories, *words, just words, Vetrov, if you don't snap back soon, all that will be left of you is a pale yellow trace of urine in the slush*, the one they are about to shoot is only the mortal coil I jettisoned a long time ago. *You're acting brave, Vetrov, how can you snap your fingers at being scared out of your mind? Neither the snow nor the clouds and the wind you like so much will join you in nothingness.*

The cockroach wriggles, nibbles, gambols. Does it sense my distress? Is it trying to get in tune with me? Is it, too, trying to slow down time? What drives it to pace up and down the blanket? And why does it suddenly head toward the floor? It progresses by sliding down the metallic foot of the bed, stops for a while before falling to land on its back under the bed where it starts fidgeting, caught up in the folds of a torn newspaper page. My cell is visited, checked and cleaned everyday; so who managed to stick this paper under my bed while I was asleep? I delicately pick up the cockroach between my thumb and my index and drop it on my pillow. I anxiously grab the newspaper, which is already several months old; it too is a mere envelope, a wrapper containing a bouquet of artificial flowers, blue roses I want to trample on but don't for fear of displaying any sign of anger that would make them too happy, I know; they keep watching me.

You're wrong in suspecting them, Vetrov, you're wrong in dismissing Svetlana's gesture. As if I could forget about the blue roses, *as if one could forget about the good life*, the years of glory, *the traveling*, the high life with everything smiling at us, *those were the good times, Vetrov, when you hummed French songs.* They had thought about everything at the KGB School, except the most important, this emotional impetus without which it is impossible to immerse oneself in a foreign language, *a dangerous liaison*, potentially pernicious, between the mother tongue and the foreign language *which gradually becomes familiar;* the French language they asked me to learn *and which you liked right away, Vetrov,* to the point that I got attached to it as one would to a mistress, *those were the good times, Vetrov, you had everything they wanted, you would blend into the background.*

Memories float around the cell, gossamer threads in the limpid autumn air. I am leaning over the parapet on the Alexander bridge, watching the sight-seeing river boats passing by. Tourists look up toward the bridge, I wave at them, they wave back; they are just passing, I am staying. Standing on the bridge, I felt from my first day in Paris that I was hand in glove with the city. *It was on October 10, Vetrov, on your birthday, you were born under Libra, a premonitory sign.* It was my first Sunday in Paris. I delighted in strolling around the capital, getting lost, standing back, finally giving myself the slip. I let go, I was no longer in control of myself and no longer feared spreading myself thin. Small fragments of me floated in the air of Paris, mingling with it, merging with it. It brought back the thrilling hide-and-seek games of my childhood. Only Paris could inspire the freedom I suddenly allowed myself. Getting free from one's self is no easy endeavor, but it's so exhilarating. Just when I thought I had lost myself along the river embankments, I got myself back in a public park. Does what you diagnosed as a split personality date back to this glorious day? *Comrade Vetrov exploded in Paris; fortunately we were there to pick up the pieces and bring them back to the homeland, Mother Russia never abandons her children.*

Who's talking about abandonment, Comrade? A Russian man I am, a Russian man I remain, caught between alternating states, but I get an ever stronger grip on myself after each lapse. The Service chose me because of my enthusiasm for life, *and because you had everything to be liked by the French,* and I did not drop my guard! *You were a good father, a good husband, a good communist.* And a vigilant agent! There was not a single moment, including during sleep, when I was not aware of being watched, conscious that my behavior was dissected, that the slightest mistake on my part would be used against me. I've always been aware of my flaws, Comrade, who doesn't have any? *A thorough, albeit late, self-criticism could redeem you in the eyes of History.* My wounds are my companions and I have learned how to turn handicaps into assets. If my sensitivity makes me vulnerable, *your heart beats too fast, Vetrov, you like parties, pretty women, expensive cars*, it also helps me probe the adversary's mind and, when exposed, vulnerability becomes a trap ensnaring the enemy. The presumptuous wolf rushes at the presumed lamb, a decoy meant to lure him and thus uncover him. The weakness of the strong, the strength of the weak. *You still remember your dialectics courses.* Knowing how to adapt to the other's game, leaving him a few feathers to save your own skin, *are you becoming reasonable*, and resurface where nobody expects you. *It is never too late to rebound*, never too late to go whale-hunting in the White Sea, to watch the Bear and the Goat dance during the Sokolniki Fair, never too late to listen to the song about the unwed mother played by a blind man on the snow violin.

What is the cockroach looking for? I thought it was content to rest on my bed, coming and going between the pillow and the white shirt, lingering on the burgundy tie, immersed in my smells, appropriating my universe. The stubborn creature went back to its hiding place, it finds the paper flowers intriguing. The virago cleaned my cell but did not touch them. As if this slattern could experience feelings resembling decency! The roach keeps rummaging about, it squeezes into interstices, scouting around, how come you didn't think about it sooner, you know eternal Russia, another white page hides under the ordinary newspaper page, with scattered letters. The letters dance a frantic kazachok under my eyes, turning kaleidoscope, *remember Vetrov the long hours deciphering*, syllables are composed, words are formed, a whole sentence emerges, *a car is waiting in front of the Praga*. Once deciphered, I mix the letters, crumple the paper into a ball and discard it into the toilet bowl.

I no longer see the roach. Could I have thrown it away inadvertently with the paper? Heartrending cries are coming from the courtyard, followed by crackling. Crackling or gun shots? *That's one dog less on the planet.* This is the kind of eulogy I'd better expect if I can't extricate myself from this pit. Somebody spits on the window of my cell. Probably some red-nosed clown, an ordinary executioner rewarded for his dirty work with two or three bottles of adulterated vodka. From the other side of the courtyard, a woman's voice strikes up the ancient tune of the Sirin, the sea bird whose song is so melancholy it enraptures ship captains and crews, letting ships drift to wreckage. "Give me a kiss, Princess, just one," answers a male voice, a voice powerful enough to move the sky and make snow fall! *You'll never get away from it, Vetrov, wherever you go, snow will find you,* how could I think I'd elude the whirling white eyes, thousands of glittering stares over the city, *looking at you through your cell window*, scrutinizing and probing the depths of my being, *you thought you could separate Russia from its winter,* I did not make the choice to go to that country with its white vast open spaces so similar to ours; *sending you to Montreal after Paris was a mistake*, my country isn't a country, it's winter, hummed the Quebec singer, and the people hummed his song in unison, and me too, *and you too*, I admit, I started humming the song, making it mine as I made that country mine; haven't I always loved snow and cold weather, and which Soviet person in my place would not have marveled at cars starting right away in hard freezing weather, at a country with no power outages, at the friendly faces of the passersby, at well-stocked stores accessible to all, at a diverse society living in harmony, *yet they were filming you, Vetrov, they were tapping your phone, following you, tracking you down;* at a time when I wondered if what I saw was dream or reality, I couldn't forget I was their enemy, I pulled myself together; which was the dream, where was reality, who was exploiting whom, I kept giving my interlocutors the answers the Party had taught me; I was simply surrounded by propaganda, at least that's what I was forcing myself to believe, but sometimes I could feel the ground shake under my feet *when Svetlana left her jewels in consignment at the jewelry store in*

Montreal without insuring them and without first checking with the local Soviet authorities; that's your version, Svetlana, my sweet, that time you were not clever enough, a lamb among wolves, *a Soviet woman in the capitalist jungle,* you thought they were more honest than we are, you were trusting, *talk about being naive,* you just wanted to have your ring repaired, but the jeweler shop "got burglarized," you'll never see the sapphire, the diamond or the emerald again, *you got carried away, Vetrov, you got infected with petit-bourgeois individualism*; true, my certitudes were crumbling, *yet we had done everything possible to protect you against the depravity inherent in a world dominated by money,* I hung in there, though, remaining, as I still do, indissolubly linked to my Soviet homeland, *spare us the hollow phrases,* we no longer speak the same language, *you turned your back on your people,* I wanted to loosen the ties, *you must pay the price,* my body already no longer belongs to me, do whatever you want with it, *we're going to annihilate it, you'll return to ashes faster than you think,* you forgot that I have, you have, we have a winged soul with fins, I'm going to dive and fly into the well of light.

Where are your wings, Vetrov, where are your fins? Where is the well of light? There is nothing, indeed, other than this reflection, this sneaky and crawling light oozing through the opening, nothing else but the relentless rumination of memories, *chewing over leads nowhere,* fruitless reverie; *what if the roach were a bird,* it could take me away to a distant land, *farther than three times nine mountains,* farther than three times nine forests, *farther than three times nine seas;* a new land, *where you could start over,* soon joined by Sveta and Vladik. *And here you are, Vetrov, as pure as snow,* having forgotten the blood on my hands, *having forgotten the treason,* but how to start again, *how to go seven leagues in one leap,* the roach is not the Sirin bird, I am not the knight with the golden keys; *you still have faithful friends,* I'd like to believe it, but who would attempt to get me out of this jail? *A car is waiting in front of the Praga.* What do they want? Do they believe I'm going to swallow it whole? Are they trying to make me believe in the existence of a network that would be so devoted to me? A great

32

many officers are aware of the sinking stagnation of our country. But how many among them would be ready to take the plunge? Could I have had followers? I'd like to believe it, but chances are too slim for me to rise to the bait. I close my fist to warm up the roach taking shelter in my palm. I sink into a liberating sleep. The car is a chariot of fire taking off from Red Square, heading for an enchanted city through which a silvery river runs.

I am hopeful again. Let's hope masks will drop, lies will go away, and the immense jail crumble. Let's hope the snow will fly freely and the wind play its music; it's been a few days since I have heard howling from the surrounding cells, rattling from the machine gun fire, or the thud of collapsing bodies. Truth has spread, light is close, Russia waits for the Spring, the czar does not forget his people, *somebody sent you flowers, Vetrov*, is now the right time to die? *Someone filed a plea for clemency.* Svetik, my precious gem, my jewel, my sapphire, my diamond, my emerald, who else, other than you, despite my vile deeds, would have attempted such a plea? *They let you write*, a rare privilege, *they gave you the opportunity to look back on your erring ways*, my last hope, *it's up to you to decide whether you can make yourself useful*, it's up to me to decide the way I want to end my life, *take your time, Vetrov, remember every detail*, to put back together the scattered pieces of the puzzle, my long stay in France and the Canadian parenthesis, *don't be afraid of repeating yourself*, five years in Paris, *this was the big turn in your life, here you were, chief-engineer*, an excellent cover allowing me to meet manufacturers, sales managers and electronics experts. *You were at the same time an office man, managing files, writing relevant memos,* and a field man, I organized missions and invitations with specialists in those sensitive areas; I conducted negotiations, rubbing elbows with the flower of French high technology, and I was invited into society. *You could be seen at Maxim's, at the Lido, Tour d'Argent;* Svetlana's Slavic charm worked wonders. She knew how, my little fox. Her manners were not Paris manners, but it didn't matter; her natural grace charmed old blasé men ready to bend over backward to facilitate the young Soviet couple's adaptation to French society. How beautiful she was, my little fox in her flaming red suit, a Moscow poppy in the Paris of the thirty-year boom that followed World War II. *You were not outdone either, Vetrov!* True, I was working relentlessly, openly and clandestinely, having a double mission, which I never forgot, I was not in Paris only for trade, I was a soldier, a pirate, a predator looking for prey to seduce, turn over, and pressure; I could reach my objectives only by infiltrating the place of my posting, immersed in the Parisian life style.

Tell us about Paris, Vetrov. The city changes according to the mood of the observer. A fickle and whimsical city, a spellbinding city with countless facets, a city where French contradictions are glaringly revealed like a caricature. Very soon, I sensed the deeply rooted tradition enduring everywhere, to the point of mortgaging the future, while they claim to deny it, even to abolish it. *French duplicity*, most certainly ambiguity, republican declarations and monarchic behaviors. The all-mighty individualist is only a petty bourgeois who pretends he wants to turn society upside down while dreaming of cultivating his garden. All I had to do was push into contradiction to obtain what I was after. *An exemplary agent, that's what you had been all those years, Vetrov, and had you remained that way you wouldn't be rotting like a rat in this squalid dump.*

Beloved grandmother with your snow-white hair, dancing in the wind that blows from the steppe, is it you? Is it your face I see in the window? Is it you coming to rescue your Volodia? Here you are, one leap and you are with me, you don't care about space and time, you abolish them both, no one knows soothing words better than you do, and here you are once again lulling your grandson, singing in his ear the song of the intrepid soldier riding his horse for days and nights through freezing deserts to reach the gold mountain. Your voice, grandmother, becomes lower, more emotional, because the soldier will never make it to the gold mountain; you know it and I know it too, yet both of us in the evening in the izba want to hope, we want to believe in a happy ending, and there are many reasons to stay hopeful; the intrepid soldier has more than one trick up his sleeve, he makes light of danger, and keeps on riding relentlessly and confidently, because he is the only one—and he knows it, and grandmother and I know it too—he is the only one who knows the passage between both worlds. But before getting there—grandmother's voice is now both soft and heart-breaking—he must go through the petrified kingdom, at great danger for himself, as it was for all the living creatures that once populated it: snakes, lizards, titbirds, red, blue and pink roses, blonde maidens with green eyes, laughing children, shepherds, princes, and even poets and musicians; yes, the danger is great for all to be turned to stone! How could the little soldier escape this fatal outcome, sighs grandmother, unless an all-mighty angel stands by him? I never found out how the tale ended because that night grandmother from Simbirsk breathed her last; I know nothing more today because the wild wind blows the snow hair far away and, with it, the intrepid soldier on his quest to find passage between both worlds. *You've been left alone, Vetrov, alone to face your life and yourself.*

They're not through wondering about Vetrov; some will keep going after his character, others will exalt him; what will be said and written about him in the near future will just be the repetition of this silent confrontation with myself in a Moscow jail. *Vetrov against Vetrov,* Vetrov torn between contradictory feelings, *and this agonizing struggle, Vetrov, started in Paris.* Actually, it was in Moscow, in my Soviet school, that I discovered the little French theater whose heroes had names: Hugo, Zola, Barbusse, Montand; where the sans-culottes interacted with Normandie-Niemen pilots, where Louise Michel and Gérard Philipe danced the Carmagnole under the benevolent eyes of grandpa Marx and uncle Lenin. "Long live France!" exclaimed the comrades before collapsing under fascist bullets at the end of the play. If France existed, it was because each generation counted a small number of valiant knights and brigands standing up to defend her or put her back on her feet. *In Moscow you dreamt of France, Vetrov, but how many Frenchmen would be ready today to die for freedom?* I was asking myself the same question when strolling the streets of Paris. How could these spoiled children have had any understanding of the feelings experienced by a Soviet citizen living in France in the late sixties? *An agent has no existential qualms, Vetrov.*

An agent is a human being. For thirty years of my life I came down on the side of the positive heroes who pushed the nihilists back into the outer darkness. In my student room, on the wall facing the bed, I posted the picture of a Soviet soldier hoisting the red flag over the Reichstag. Everything was clear then, Evil on one side, black like the swastika, Good on the other, red like blood, like life, like the rising sun, *like Svetlana's suit,* she was going around boutiques, crazy about perfumes, jewelry, Paris cars, *the black Peugeot, was it for her that you sold your soul, Vetrov?* Vetrov the trafficker, the huckster, the wheeler-dealer, Vetrov who, in Paris, dreamt of becoming a petit-bourgeois, Vetrov the visionary, the libertarian, the friend of France, one and the other, one or the other, they're all wrong, they're all right: Vetrov is a man torn between contradictory passions, love and hatred, loving hate for both Paris and Russia.

The snow flakes are getting thicker, pushed by a damp wind, they stick to the cell window. *Nothing of what's going on in Vetrov's heart escapes them.* They ignore nothing of my past, they worm their way into my heart of hearts, reading my thoughts. We refused to see that the utopia was turning into a nightmare, we refused to take responsibility for our mistakes, to acknowledge our weaknesses and remedy them, we are going to pay for it dearly. *You're a bird of ill omen, Vetrov,* a madman, a clairvoyant, *a troubled personality, and it's in Paris that you broke free;* it was in Paris that I understood the world was neither white nor black, that evil and good are closely intermingled in each country, in every human being, *Vetrov against Vetrov,* love and hatred inextricably linked. God alone knows how I hated this fickle city, which offers herself to all—here goes the merry-go-round: Russian Paris, Arab Paris, Indian Paris, ever-so-fashionable Paris, many-colored Paris, popular, proletarian Paris, bourgeois Paris, mirror, mirage, make-believe, capital of tricks and evil spells that lured me like it did so many others. *You're admitting to it, Vetrov, shout, yell your confession out for all to hear in this prison.* Yes, I let myself be taken in, like all the others, provincials from France and elsewhere, peasants from the Danube and the Volga, whom the coquette eyed scornfully after having seduced them. Yes, I hate you, Paris, with loving hatred, *spout your hatred,* I hate your pretensions, imposing your enlightenment to the world, I hate your smugness and your arrogance. You're never wrong, you always fit in. You still believe you're it, you're reassuring yourself, you're having a facelift, you're gloating, you hail the millions of foreign passersby who come for window-shopping, but at dusk, when one cannot distinguish a dog from a wolf, in the November evenings, you're no longer so self-confident. Where have the men of breeding and the freethinkers gone? And what happened to French politeness? Things change, days go by, your voice is starting to quaver, but it is when she is just past her prime that a woman is the most attractive. *And that's when you fell into her arms?* As strange as it may seem coming from a Soviet agent shielded against all emotions, I was first seduced by the language, fluid with free liaisons, a wheedling language, as soft as it is precise, with words that will delight me until my last day—nobody can forbid me to do that—turning them in my mouth, making them slide on my tongue just as one savors an old armagnac; *you're not the only one whose head has been turned by Paris, Vetrov; since you dream of writing, since you want so much to be talked about, here is a great theme for sensitive souls, a schmaltzy story,* the poor muzhik riding a wooden rooster, taking off toward the sunset, effortlessly flying and flying over hundreds of versts and landing at the top of the Eiffel tower, *falling madly in love with Paris to the point of selling his soul to her,* of giving her his heart.

How could it be a crime to love the most beautiful city in the world? Why this universal distrust? From which troubling abyss, from what iron age comes this complex of encirclement, this persecution mania which generates a pathological susceptibility to exclude everything that differs from us? *You're the pathological one, Vetrov.* Where is the doctor? When is the radical cure to be expected? *You're the one who is sick.* I am sick from wanting to breathe, to open a window to the world? *Hatred blinds you, Vetrov, you can no longer see the Russian people as they are.* That's all I see, the goodness of the Russian people, those millions of simple men and women humiliated, tormented, tortured, so much so that I envy you, little roach; you have more freedom than the Homo Sovieticus, you do not need a residency permit, you come and go at will according to your mood! Instead of studying electronics, I would have been better advised to devote my life to observing you; Russia is the paradise of cockroaches, by now I would have become an internationally renowned specialist, *dictyoptera* would have no secrets left for me, *the name of Vetrov linked forever to blattoptera,* but I went astray, *you didn't pull it off,* I lost my way, *from hunter you became the game*; and here I am, down to envying you, little roach. *It could teach you a lot about tracking, dodging, passing,* it is at home in dark and damp nooks and crannies, *it knows how to get oriented in the heart of a maze,* it perfected to an extreme the art of hiding in narrow cracks, *it knows perfectly the difference between right and left,* with its sensitive bristles it can detect the faintest smells and sounds, *quick and agile, it easily escapes its pursuers,* it was one of my first playmates in grandmother's izba in Simbirsk. While snow flakes were eddying outside the window, perched at the top of the pechka, lying in its warmth, I watched a roach coming and going on the wooden icon, from Adam to Eve and from Eve to Adam to stop eventually on the snake's head. And each time grandmother, whose silhouette I could barely make out in the dark room, and who had silently followed the blatta orientalis's comings and goings from the beginning, would warn me against the snake's guile.

Why did the soldier prefer going to hell rather than to heaven? Where is the red rooster which will take me to the Eiffel tower? Why do the Russians dream of catching hold of the snow violin? You're no longer here, grandmother, to answer my questions! Now is hardly the time to sink into dreams. There is bustling in the corridor, the screeching of the gates, the upsetting grating of massive keys in locks, one, two, three doors opening, hurried steps, time freezes, breathing stays suspended in the chest, *the die is cast, Vetrov, all you'll have been is a piece of bait meant to attract the big cats, you made a mistake listening to the sirens of the West,* I was wrong to keep cultivating my difference, *you fooled nobody, the dice were loaded;* what would grandmother think, what would she say about my tribulations? *How would she judge your volte-face?* Who will have the last word, the roach or the snake? *Your turn has come, Vetrov!* The time is near when the huge nonsense, the illusion of the big night will burst like a soap bubble, Russia, *this old whore, as you call it,* not without affection—she gave a lot of herself but she is getting tired, it's time to leave the job to others, *your turn has come, Vetrov,* the communists no longer speak in one voice, the power centers are multiplying, Tito, Albania and, above all, China, are no longer taking orders from Moscow, the South started following new paths, the West lost none of its appeal, *you were wrong Vetrov, wrong at being right too soon,* an unforgivable wrong, *some must die for others to live,* the slaughterhouse is an essential link of the chain, *do you hear the clanking, Vetrov? One, two, three doors being shut back,* hurried steps, the breath one tries to hold? Do the calf or the lamb lament on the way to the slaughterhouse?

What are those sudden cries? I can't believe my ears, these are cries of joy! *Early release.* I had lost hope, says one, the people's justice is kind, says the other, *we are not brutes, Vetrov,* no you're not, you're ordinary people, *as you were, as you still are, Vetrov,* an ordinary man, a child listening to grandmother's folk tales in the izba, a good son, a good husband who wants to see the blue roses again, a good father who wants to pick chanterelles with Vladik again, *things change, Vetrov,* time is short, *the old stories about double agents in leather coats and fedoras exchanging briefcases at the Friedrich-Strasse station will no longer entertain people, now's your chance,* it's for me to decide. What do you think, grandma? *It's up to you to choose the roses of blood on the white shirt,* or long peaceful years in the found-again coziness of Svetlana's sitting room, *think about yourself, think about them, Vetrov,* I reflect about the warrior

39

who thought he could defeat death, *now is not the time for the philosopher*, the cries of joy can be heard again, *three free men met by their families outside the prison*, is the bad dream going away? Is a last-minute pardon possible? A stroke of luck, it would not be the first time that spies are exchanged on the Potsdam bridge. *What do you think, Vladimir Ippolitovich?*

I think of Russia, disfigured and tattered, I think of the stagnating water in puddles, the stench of sour cabbage in staircases, the gloomy faces of the passersby hugging the walls and waiting for hours in the cold until a store opens that has nothing to offer; I think of the violin that vanishes as soon as you try to catch hold of it, and I think, shaking all over, of all those bonds that unite me to my country.

There is a message for you from your old friend who did not forget you, they said you'd understand. This time, the message is clear, in case I would not have deciphered the text hidden in the bouquet of blue roses. A car is waiting in front of the Praga. He waited for me only once in front of the popular restaurant. I told him that the place was too conspicuous; after that, I was the one setting the rendezvous locations. What game is the warder going along with? It's unthinkable that he could have been manipulated by my old friend. Who would believe that such an operation could succeed in the heart of Moscow? He's certainly capable of anything. *You're dithering, Vetrov, you've always been dithering, on one side one day, on the other side the next day, make up your mind, don't delay*, a last chance, is it possible? *Straight is the gate*, the eye of a needle, *watch the roach, take your cue from it*, this whole story sounds like a blatant lie, all the same, the guy managed to confuse me. He was careful to give the message at a time when his stooge was busy somewhere else. As soon as she's back, he pretends indifference. But now, she's the one who changes roles. Here she is bringing me borsch the way I like it, red and steamy, cooked Svetlana-style. What's come over them? Are they trying to make the French, *braggarts who think they can fool us a second time*, believe that they can exfiltrate me and, as I climb up the airplane gangway, I'll be given an ultimatum. *It's up to you, Vetrov, France or Switzerland, plastic surgery, and the merry-go-round starts turning again.* What about the airplane ticket and the passport? *You should know that it's only a formality!* You want me to betray myself? *It wouldn't be the first time.* But how to live with myself? *You'll get used to it.* What about Svetlana and Vladik, they'll follow me? *They will if you prove yourself to be cooperative, this time we'll keep an eye on you,* but aren't you forgetting the deconditioning I worked on so eagerly, this long effort to be able to live true to myself at last? Now that I have freed myself from my armor, that the scales fell from my eyes and that I see myself as I am, and the world as it is, do you believe I can go back that easily? *We're not the ones asking, think of the white shirt, we're not barbaric, Vetrov!* What are you expecting of me then, that you don't already know? *A point still escapes us, the only one left which our experts in psychological mechanistics,* the thin-lipped man, *want to clarify,* illuminate; *what we want is to identify with precision the moment when the course of your life started to change, when you lost control over yourself,* that moment when I escaped at last from my own vigilance, *others no longer recognized you,* I was no longer myself, as Ludmila said, *the moment when you crossed to the other side,* but does such a precise moment, does this breaking point exist? You are running after me to no avail, you're trying to grab me, but I eluded you again, I am no longer on your side nor on the other side, *none of those who attempted to cross through the passage between worlds ever returned.*

The method is classic, they blow hot and cold, the warder and the old hag are no longer paying attention to me, they are sharing a bottle of pure alcohol without even offering me a single shot. Those morons are not without knowledge of basic reflexes. *Your life hangs by a thread.* Despite the fact that I used those techniques myself, weakened as I am by the endless questioning, the harsh living conditions in the penitentiary camp, the pain of all those tragic events—the responsibility of which is mine alone—and the tremendous tension preceding my arrest, I am close to falling in with this new game they want me to play, as long as the nightmare stops, *the sentence is not irrevocable, Vetrov,* the hag's tone is almost amicable, *a last confidence*, the pearl of pearls, *the ultimate secret*, the Vetrov mystery, *for a plate of sprats*, the ones I like best, with their golden shimmering, *canned for export*, they melt in the mouth, *with a flask of vodka, Vetrov, from the Director*; but what is it you want to learn that you don't already know, after having filled seven volumes of revelations in the archives of the Committee for State Security; don't tell me that you, the champions of materialism, believe in mystery, *the mystery of the Russian soul, now here is a topic for you, Vetrov*, an inexhaustible one, what do you think, little roach? And you, grandmother, what do you think?

Grandmother understood nothing about platitudes, and brushed aside hollow sounding words like the alleged mystery of the Russian soul. In her opinion, all mankind is treated in the same way, all children of Adam and Eve, all ready to devour the apple if presented to them from the right side, ruby-red and succulent, whereas the other side is still green and tough. Where is the straight and narrow path, grandmother? You are no longer here to tell me! What is there to choose between the inevitability of death and the desire to live? The young pioneer singing patriotic songs around the campfire in the Valdai forest did not experience doubt. Like the soldier replacing the swastika flag with the red flag at the top of the Reichstag, he knew then what was good, what was wrong, *you knew Vetrov, you both knew, Svetlana and you, when you arrived in Paris*; I didn't doubt, we didn't doubt, the world was at our feet, Paris was about to offer herself to us.

The crackling of larch twigs merges with the scratching of the roach against the paper. The past keeps spinning with the present. *The past sticks to your skin, Vetrov*, the past I tried to unchain myself from, *and this Paris that bewitched you, the charmer let himself be charmed.*

Who let oneself be charmed? Who fell into the other's arms? Who was more than willing to sell oneself? *The Vetrovs are artists, acrobats who always land on their feet.* Magicians with more than one trick up their sleeves. Two or three kilos of caviar here, *a precious icon there*, along with a generous distribution of whiskey, and a round of drinks, no one will be the wiser, *you open the trunk of the Peugeot* in the underground garage, *between well-mannered people there is always a way to come to an agreement*, a TV set for me, *another one for the Resident*, a satellite radio for the ambassador, *a Dior's purse for Madame*, everyone is happy, *business is business*, you shut the trunk back, everyone exchanges business cards, *Svetlana smiles*, please stop by for a drink, *those Soviets who were generally believed to be barbaric are positively charming people*; we could be their fellow travelers for a little bit, just to try, a zest of adventure, putting just the little finger in the system, *it's a real thrill*; no... we wouldn't go as far as a grand alliance, two or three lucrative and mutually advantageous contracts, one or two technology transfers paid cash on the barrel and, to celebrate, let's all meet at the Alcazar! Oh, please! Accept our invitation, with Svetlana of course, who looks so pretty in her little red suit, so becoming, *everything's hunky-dory, Vetrov, between you and Paris, it was a honeymoon, you were following in the steps of your illustrious predecessors; in Moscow, at the Center, they were proud of you!*

Naturally, I knew of the successful recruiting by our Service, *three big fish caught in our nets*, a deputy secretary of Foreign Affairs, a retired officer and the boss of a large nationalized company.

With the diplomat, it had been slow going. Under a modest appearance, the deputy secretary hid a shameless ambition. The lower level competitive exam he had passed would never allow him to become an ambassador. He had conceived a lingering hatred toward the authorities of that state, too elitist for his liking. For a year, the young man had contented himself with giving us background notes about the overall atmosphere, analyses of the political landscape of his country. *Those who intend to submit France to the Anglo-Saxon model, allowing for the changeover of political power by two major parties, are ignorant of our traditions. For many years to come, there will be three leftwing currents—bourgeois, anarchist and Caesarean, and three rightwing currents—liberal, Bonapartist and legitimist.* It's only later that we could obtain from the diplomat a few spicy biographies of senior officials and, most of all, copies of dispatches sent from Moscow by the French ambassador.

As for the company CEO, that man had something to be ashamed of. The heroic partisan's past that led him to his post was, in fact, a sham. A civil servant under Vichy, the man had zealously executed orders, *going as far as having Gaullists, Communists and Jews arrested*. He had been careful not to leave any written trace of his actions. On the other hand, he made sure to build a solid dossier documenting the double game he allegedly played for the benefit of free France. *That was not counting on the Gestapo's archives recovered in Berlin by the Red Army and gone over with a fine-tooth comb by our snoopers.* As soon as we produced damning evidence of his collaboration with the Vichy regime, the man showed greater understanding. Thanks to him, Moscow obtained the operational plans for the national railroads, the energy grid, and the main French ports.

We had a certain reluctance, even some embarrassment, manipulating the Normandie–Niemen veteran. The retired colonel was a dedicated friend to his combat comrades. Was it a reason to break him? The officer was experiencing a critical stage of his life. His pregnant mistress wanted an abortion, which in those days was illegal in France. *After offering him assistance, the Service we had entrusted with the operation, in a brother country, had blackmailed the unfortunate man.* Was it established that the former hero, in dire straits, delivered in bulk the drawings of several nuclear power plants and detailed information about the new engine of the French aircraft carrier?

I had not followed closely any of those cases but I had got wind of them. The recruiting of the Normandie–Niemen hero had left bitter memories. *Vetrov, the sentimental!* It wasn't an even playing field. Democracies laid their cards on the table, but we did not hesitate to use underhand tricks. *Imperceptibly, Comrade Vetrov yielded to the enemy's magic spell.* Comrade Vetrov observed French society, compared both worlds, and the comparison was not in favor of the Soviet state and the socialist economy. Not by a long shot. But as long as I was a member of our Residency in Paris, it was out of the question to let any of my new feelings show.

The dissociation process had begun. By becoming estranged from your family, you were about to break with yourself; one needs first to step away in order to be able to sort oneself out, and then reconnect with oneself. This mutation that a single man submits himself to is the same mutation the entire nation will have to go through in order to avoid falling again into the illusory snare of myths. *Vetrov, all you are is a minuscule leaf swirling in the wind; like the muzhik who got locked up by his parrot, you let your double imprison you;* it's a dangerous combat that each man must have with himself, *a combat from which you emerged in tatters. Who was the real Vetrov during those Paris years, the one who saw the positive side of the foreign experience or the one who surrendered to the sirens of bourgeois decadence?*

The recruiting of an engineer with access to the manufacturing secrets of the French space launchers by the other Vetrov, *ours,* was an achievement that should have thrust him to the top of the hierarchy. Yes, I too was one of the champions of large-scale plundering. Without us, *without you, Vetrov, we have a very good memory,* the Soviet Union would not have equipped itself so fast with space laser weapons or the electromagnetic launcher. *And thanks to you and a few other exceptional agents, we acquired the capability to detect the enemy's nuclear submarines!*

Viewed from here, in this prison, how far away and vain all this seems! Immense efforts reduced to nothing. All that remains from this fairy-tale enterprise is the sound of brooms, brushes and buckets at the bottom of a Moscow dungeon. The scrubbing squad executes the orders barked curtly by the hag who is strutting about in the corridor, scoffing at one or the other, shouting at the warder and planting herself in front of my cell.

Honorable comrade Vetrov Vladimir Ippolitovich! The Party Committee hierarchy and its leadership are sending you their cordial congratulations on the occasion of the fiftieth anniversary of the founding of our institution, and express their deep gratitude for the exceptional services you performed during many years. We wish you and your family health and success in your future undertakings for the greatest good of our venerable homeland.

In the surrounding cells, inmates guffaw. Not all inmates can pride themselves on such a record of achievements. *They aren't all turncoats like you, Vetrov.* The harridan's coarse voice and sneering tone hit home. She takes delight in rubbing salt in the wound with her red podgy fingers. Does she expect to persuade me to become once again the man I was at the time, when my merits justified such congratulations?

Well deserved praise, Vetrov! Certainly, I had accumulated successes, recruited several moles, identified potential defectors, made friends in the Parisian smart set, was appreciated by the Resident; *but some were on the lookout for a faux pas on your part, Vetrov,* everything seemed so easy in Paris. Paris, the siren. Had I dropped my guard, had I begun adopting a middle-class perspective? *You allowed yourself to be dazzled, Vetrov, for you it was all smoke and mirrors; it started with a mundane lunch in a restaurant,* then an outing to the countryside with Svetlana, *your friend Jacques was supposed to lure you,* and through him our trade exchanges developed, *a fruitful collaboration that ended poorly for you, Vetrov,* I have no regrets, it was bound to happen, Jacques had no part in it, he didn't walk out on me, *quite the contrary, he had you in his grips and he was just the first link in the chain,* Jacques was a pleasant, quick-witted man, *with an easy-going directness: they always send the nice guy to scout around;* it's in times of hardship that ones counts his friends, if he hadn't been there for me when I had the accident, *the black Peugeot hit by another car which disappeared* before I could write down the plate number, *you had had one drink too many Vetrov;* it's Jacques, called to for help, who had the car fixed, *and at the embassy no one ever knew about it,* he is the one who got me out of this tight corner, *if it weren't for him you'd still be one of ours Vetrov; an accident can be set up.* And there is always a nice guy showing up to help you out of your predicament and to snatch you from the clutches of the bad guys, *you don't know how right you are,* you're the ones who have been harping on about your interpretation of the facts, *you're the one contradicting yourself, one version erases the previous one,* you've interrogated me hundreds of times on this event, harassed me; you found flaws in my account of the events, so I can no longer distinguish what's true from what isn't: your multiple versions cross theirs, and I don't know where I stand anymore, *well put Vetrov,* you deadened my mind, *you're switching roles, your French friends are the ones who administered a potion without your knowing about it;* who manipulated whom? *Who else apart from your Parisian buddies would have an interest in imagining such a tale,* it was just a trivial accident, no more no less, *and if you were right, Vetrov, however much you try to act important, inflating yourself like the frog of the fable, your entire story is just a succession of meaningless incidents.*

What if I were going along with your interpretation? A buddy helps you out of an awkward position, nothing to fuss about! *It would not have been an issue if your friend Jacques had not reappeared years later.* A trivial event, Comrade, pure coincidence, if Vetrov is just a frog, why not throw him back into the river? If you locked me up, it's because you thought I was dangerous. You understood nothing about Vetrov, *we're missing a few clues,* that's the least you can say, all you saw in him is the sensualist, *Vetrov the multifaceted socialite,* and I passed up none of the pleasures Paris life had to offer; *then why didn't you choose what your kind calls freedom?* The French did not understand it either when I turned down their offer to stay. *To tell the truth, it's Svetlana who turned it down.* Yes, Svetlana my little fox, you were right, you wanted to be on Russian soil again, and it was in Moscow that I wanted in my deepest being to choose freedom, to decide about my future, that is. *Antisocial behavior, pernicious deviance, such was our experts' diagnostic to characterize this point.*

The roach flipped on its back just like a cat would. Is it going to purr? Is that its way to ask for some petting? At the first light touch, it quivered with pleasure. An ocher light filters through the small window where a few snowflakes are fluttering about.

Choosing freedom. Would I have made this choice if I hadn't spent, quite by chance and remaining incognito, an entire evening under a cedar tree in the park of a pink villa? *Strange, you didn't mention it during interrogations*, how could you have understood since you believe only in confrontation, cold war, power struggle, class struggle?

"Paris is Soviet!" He had slightly raised his voice and emphasized his statement with a resounding laugh. It seemed to me, then, that he was talking to me rather than to the interlocutor facing him, to me whom he had never met, to me who had been sitting a few meters away behind him for ten minutes or so. *How could he have not been aware of your presence!* At the time, I knew nothing about him, but among the fifteen or twenty people strolling about in the park, he was the only one who attracted my attention, not because of his physique, although noticeable, but because of some invisible, mysteriously empathetic power emanating from him. I then was certain that, subconsciously if not fully aware, he had sensed the power of attraction he had over me, *with no attempt on your part to oppose any resistance*, and froze me on my seat. *Consummate skills!* While clearly speaking to the person in front of him, P was making sure all his words would resonate in me.

"Paris is Soviet!" Making a point to be doubly attentive to his friend whom I could see face-on, as if trying to cut short the silent impulse carrying me toward him, he indicated on an imaginary map a series of points scattered throughout the city: the Aeroflot offices, the Black Sea insurance company, the headquarters of the Communist Party Place du Colonel Fabien, Intourist, the Tass Agency, the Bank for Northern Europe, Sovexportfilm, the France-USSR Association and of course the heart of the system, the Soviet embassy Boulevard Lannes, and more specifically the Residency occupying the three upper stories of the embassy, turned into an echo-free chamber, *accessible only by the officers of the Service*. The two men had exchanged a few more words in hushed tones and then walked away toward the far end of the park.

Before completely burning away, a big log had collapsed, broken in the middle at the center of the campfire. The red and golden sparks glowing in the dark danced with grace in the peaceful evening air.

A textbook case, a muffled and sideways attack, a model of subliminal approach. He had already ensnared you without your being aware of it. You're the only one to believe you were there incognito.

And what if they were right? What do you think, grandmother? The wolf didn't realize how cunning the fox was, worse, he gave credence to the fox's tall stories. "Put your tail into an ice hole, move it slowly back and forth, and you'll catch all the fish you want," was the fox's advice. And the next morning, the gullible wolf, surprised by the villagers who had come to catch him, could escape only by leaving his tail behind, in the ice hole.

Russian folk tales are the wisdom of the earth, you should have trusted them, Vetrov, you wouldn't have surrendered to the spells woven against you in the pink villa.

The fire had been rekindled under the cedar tree. The summer had been chilly, and at the end of August days were already getting shorter. A gentle breeze played with the flames, making faces appear and disappear. A pleasant phantasmagoria that took me back to the campfires of my childhood in the Valdai forests. I didn't know a soul in that place where I was for the first time, but I felt it was a trustworthy environment, no cameras, no microphones, no hefty fellow at the entrance asking me for my papers, *you have to be nice if you want something*, everyone was free to say what she or he wanted to say, anyone could come and listen, the pink villa was accessible to all, and people were free to take part or not in the conversations. They were all so excited by this exchange of ideas—crazy, sparkling, profound and, at times, funny ideas, funny enough to cause a few people to be doubled up with laughter—that nobody paid attention to me, standing there drinking in their words, and trying as much as possible to catch and absorb what was being said.

The roach has settled on my neck, right on the vocal cords, as if it wanted, through its sensitive bristles, to be penetrated by the vibrations and thus assimilate my thoughts. Does it sense that last-minute revelations could save us?

As for P, he was coming and going between the groups. *How did he manage to make that body of his, so massive and heavy, almost transparent?*

"Brezhnev is not Stalin, Stalin is not Lenin, Lenin is not Marx, true there have been, and there still are injustices, that's the price to pay, despite all the errors, Communism brings a dream…" P had stopped by a small circle of students who still believed in the utopia of the century. The discussion seemed from another era. In an attempt at opening their eyes, P touched on the climate of fear existing from Berlin to Vladivostok while the young scatterbrains kept drumming the Popular Front old tunes. Clearly impressed by P's quiet self-confidence, they had eventually admitted that violence, even state sponsored, was not the best way to attain social justice, but they refused nevertheless to recognize that before sharing the cake, you had to bake it! P had the nerve to call our regimes, which he loathed, "red fascism," and he would say it in his same quiet way, such that one of the most indoctrinated students came very close to considering him a leftover partisan of the Legion of French Volunteers Against Bolshevism!

"Uncle" Kolya at that moment clapped in the same way you would do to calm puppies playing too rough. And all was back to order. The mission P had made his in life, which was to serve the free world, *the so-called free world, Vetrov,* seemed so anachronistic to those young people that they were more amused than exasperated by it. Now, who was behind the times, who sensed the threat we represented to democracies, who else if not men of P's caliber? *You took the bait, Vetrov, caught like a fish!* Actually, I no longer doubt that P was an agent, and he did not try to conceal it, *it was no longer necessary for him to hide.* A critical moment, no doubt. *You got that right, the trial of strength had started, things could have gone one way or the other; the contradictions of capitalism had reached a crucial point, you were among those who could have contributed to its fall, and you missed the boat, Vetrov, a mistake the Soviet people, although lenient, will have a hard time forgiving.*

On the other side of the fire, the conversation between P and his interlocutor got going again. "What made you want to join the East?" asked P. "Because on the other side of the wall, dyed-in-the-wool communists have long disappeared," the young man answered, with this dark humor he learned from the people over there, ours.

"Ours," Vetrov, how dare you claim you are one of ours! However hard you try to amputate the rotten limb, which you've never stopped doing since you seized power, you won't be able to prevent gangrene from spreading to the entire Soviet body. *You're either with us, or against us!* I did not defect, I wanted to come back to my country, more than ever I assert and proclaim my Russian identity, more than ever, from my Moscow prison cell, I consider myself to be an integral, albeit minuscule, part of the empire of cockroaches. *You're insulting the people, Vetrov, you're making things worse for yourself!*

The roach, in sympathy with my moods, shows its disagreement by puffing up. It seems to be convulsed with laughter. Could *dictyoptera* be the only living creatures, besides human beings, capable of getting a kick out of a tragic situation? It climbs back up to my face, works its way through the stubbles of my beard, stops on my cheek. We are now united. The time has come to seal this union. It starts with a slight tingling sensation which, past the first surprise, could even become pleasant. The tingling diminishes, becomes gentler. The little scamp is taking advantage of the situation. The roach is giving me kisses, the words come out spontaneously and, elated, I struck up a ditty, a Paris tune. *That's right, sing, Vetrov, all is not lost, relax!*

Loosen up from what? In the park of the pink villa, discussions were of no consequence. Those were just merry brawls ending with songs. P himself was expert at easing the tense atmosphere. "When was the last time I had a good laugh? A week ago? One month, two? Impossible to remember! Democracies are gloomy. Pointless chattering, endless whining, it's the government's fault if my wife left me, if I got the flu, if it's hot, if it's cold, if it rains, if it doesn't rain, if I was born, if I'm dead! The fools have the floor! Enough to bore you to tears. The best way to make people laugh is to give them a fright! Long live absolutism! Long live dictatorship!"

A taste for paradox, *subtle provocation*, which, I was certain, was targeting me. P was not naive regarding democracy, the shortcomings of which I had observed myself. What was more of a surprise to me was the sharpness of his perception, his ability to grasp what was the best in us, the red laughter, the liberating humor. Is it necessary to erect walls and put up barbed wire for humans to start laughing?

And lo and behold, suffused with a golden glow, the face of the poet appears again. Until the end of time, facing the firing squad, he will refuse the blindfold and will gently smile at his executioners. *He who laughs last laughs best, Vetrov.* The poet's smile is stronger than death, Comrades!

The poet's smile froze forever, shattered in the noise of the bullets. Who's going to win? The weakness of the strong, the strength of the weak. The snow-haired little soldier who remembers the nights spent counting the stars or the sticky-eyed warder with her foul breath? *Think of the squirts of blood on the white shirt, remember the maid, Maria Danilovna, remember the warmth of camaraderie at the cafeteria, and don't forget the car waiting for you in front of the Praga,* nor the grudges, the stench of sour cabbage, potholes, shaky manhole covers, the guy standing watch in front of grayish housing blocks, *the plea for clemency, remember, Vetrov,* Adam and Eve on the icon in the izba, *remember the cat from Kazan, feel the snow, the clouds and the wind, remember hands touching in the midst of the new foliage of a birch grove, think of Moscow poppies,* the pink villa, the man with the small red suitcase in Paris streets; *tell us about this unique evening,* a divertimento, *a fugue,* an enchantment, *tell us about the magician whose wand led another adventurer through the passage between worlds.*

They were now talking in hushed voices, and as the night progressed, confidences became more intimate. "*Eine Kleine Ostmuzik,* little serenade from the East. Ritornello for hurdy-gurdy. I carried on, singing my favorite melodies, *The*

52

Third Man Theme which, the minute I heard the first few bars, aroused in me the dark desire to cross the border; *Lily Marlene*, a melancholy lullaby that never left me when I stayed in West Berlin, oasis of capitalism, brothel in the heart of the German Democratic Republic; and above all, *Lara's Song*. We had just watched the cranes flying. A new breeze was softly blowing from the East. Sakharov was advocating intellectual freedom. With the publishing of *Doctor Zhivago*, hope was running high. Were all the church bells throughout Russia about to announce the Resurrection? *Lara's Song* alone contains all the dreadful and tender tunes in what I call my Eastern Opera..."

"Nothing to see, nothing to hope, and all of a sudden joyous cracks when you no longer expect them, winter is not forever as we thought it was. The Russian language shimmers with caressing words to tell of the encounter, the face-to-face meeting with someone we were unknowingly waiting for."

In Meudon's blue night, P and his friend were talking but I could not distinguish who was saying what, as if they had the power to erase, in this very place, by the magic of words, the dividing line that had split Europe by decree, forty years earlier in Yalta.

Another scene, same scriptwriter, ingenious stratagem, patient and subtle approaches, the French are artists.

There are rare moments in life that defy time. Under the cedar tree the fire was dying slowly. There was an awkward silence believed to be an angel flying by, but no, "it's a militiaman," said Kolya ironically. The time had come for the French teacher, who was just back from the Eastern bloc, to open his heart. The German female students were all ears. The Japanese's violin was silent, and P was invisible.

"Am I Russia-sick like one gets lovesick? I never liked those kitschy Russian bars in Paris where everything—music, costumes, food, and even vodka—seemed to me, rightly or wrongly, phony. I know from Custine's Letters that the Russians have been, throughout their history, masters of disguise, building Potemkin villages to hide misery and hardship. And I cannot forget that, one day, Lara went out never to return, I cannot forget that her fate was the same as the fate of millions of Soviet citizens, and later millions of Eastern Europeans, arrested, exiled, assassinated. I know all this. I have all the reasons in the world to loathe Russia, but for a long time I've kept hanging around her, and each time I thought I was through with her, some event would occur that rekindled the attraction."

The Japanese had left with his violin, and the German students had fallen asleep on the bare ground, while the angel was fluttering above the fire before flying around the cedar tree several times to disappear in the sky where there was no more trace of the militiaman. Already the city was livening up, and the domes of the Sacré-Cœur were whitening in the distance.

That was the night when you started believing in angels, Vetrov, the night when I realized I had always believed in angels. The angel flying above the campfire was grandmother's angel, the one in the tales told in the izba, the angel who was the only one capable of helping the intrepid soldier escape from the petrified city. *Russia is not a fairy, Vetrov, but it's not a witch either,* the Russian people did not achieve metamorphosis, *the Russians are not devils,* they're not angels either, they have wings but cannot fly! If I like the roach so much, *it's because it too is condemned to rot in its cesspool,* it has not completed its transformation either, *but it's not aware of its fate,* how do you know that? We are more similar than you think, *you don't have wings, you can't fly away,* you're forgetting the power of the mind, soon the wind will blow and your walls will fall down.

How did a properly trained Party executive, an agent of Vetrov's caliber, let himself be contaminated by the opium of the masses? I was miles away from asking myself such a question. I was feeling good and it was enough. At most, I could have asked myself how the Fathers who ran Saint-Georges were able to ensure peace and harmony between the people who gathered there, even if only for one day. I was wrong to believe that this evening was just a parenthesis in my Parisian life. Of course I kept performing my activities as a Soviet agent on assignment in an enemy country, but I would often think back about shreds of conversation and, little by little, I realized that the park, the cedar tree, the dying fire, the pink villa had become familiar companions to the extent that they haunted me, *like you were haunted by P's heavy yet light, earthly yet ethereal figure.*

Vetrov the possessed! Quite the contrary, far from enslaving me, the persistent softness of memories invited me to think that another world, a different view of life, were possible, and that disagreements could be expressed without terrorizing, torturing, and annihilating the adversary. What did they have in common, the communist students, the young women from Berlin who claimed they were Guevarists and Trotskyites, Tolstoy the white Russian, the two Brits always volunteering to do the dishes, the Japanese and his violin, the lady connoisseur of icons who didn't understand a thing in political debates, and the small group of obligatory spongers, hysterics and alcoholics one cannot avoid at Russian parties? The fact remains that this microcosm managed to exist peacefully.

That's what the "uncles" and "aunties," and all the good Fathers at the pink villa, deluded you into believing. As if I could have been that naive! You don't teach me what hides behind Peace movements and slogans promoting East-West rapprochement. Smoke screens behind which each side continues the arms race; nobody perfected the art of propaganda like we did! *Alright, Lieutenant Colonel Vetrov, you were in good hands, but others were more cunning than you.* As if I could have let friars mislead me! *Let's talk about your friars, didn't you know that one of them was translating Solzhenitsyn, while the other wrote about Shalamov,* that all loved and spread Russian language and culture. All had a high opinion of Russian spirituality, *they were your adversaries, Vetrov,* I had no doubt about that but I respected them, *Vatican agents, Vetrov,* just one detachment of Swiss Guards, a minuscule state, with an unarmed man at its head, who scares you so much you attempted to assassinate Him! In the end, the mind wins over the sword, comrades, and it's quite possible that the notion of the existence of another order of things came to me that night under the cedar tree. Is this order any different from the one my grandmother initiated me into?

Does that necessarily mean that I must be sentenced? Was Lobachevsky sentenced for having invented a different geometry? I was one of the best positioned in the entire Soviet Union to know and precisely evaluate our industrial power, our military arsenal, our scientific potential, and the data I had access to allowed me to make a similar evaluation of American power. As the evening in Meudon drew to a close, I became aware that with this mad arms race the world was heading for disaster. *You stalled, Vetrov,* that's right, the word is accurate, stalling and transitioning to this other plane from which one considers the situation from a different standpoint. Everything that I had taken seriously until then became pointless!

It stopped snowing, the faint glimmer from the snowflakes comes in gracefully through the window, flowing into the cell where it revives the inscriptions on the walls, left by previous prisoners, giving life to the pale blue paper roses. It is like a reflection of early childhood's white mornings and of the embraces in the clearings of the Valdai forests. Recalling the evening in Meudon—and it's not the least of its powers—helps me reconnect with my distant past, linking it to my present.

But for goodness sake, this Saint-Georges, Vetrov, where you claim you had your Epiphany, surely you know it was a breeding-ground of anti-Soviet people, always fighting among themselves and looking back nostalgically to the old regime, a shelter for white guards; yeah, I know the old song for I sang it myself, *but you made sure not to report about what you saw and heard that evening.* Yes, I was careful not to because what was being said under the cedar tree was contained within a magic circle, timeless and outside the scope of my assignment.

You thought you'd reached the shores of a new world, Vetrov, whereas you were just an ordinary victim of an illusion engineered by a sorcerer, that night you became someone else, you were a plaything in his hands.

Freedom is a fruit you cannot forego once you've tasted it,

but how can we, the Russian people, feel nostalgic for a treasure we've never had?

"Years, many long years, spent in the East trying to open up the iron curtain, however little it may be, trying to drill minute holes in the ice, with infinite patience, unflinching perseverance, but also in dreadful solitude, obliged to hold one's tongue, to stay vigilant at all times," such was the young French teacher's experience of our society as told to P, who listened to this life story while rearranging the logs in the fire and rekindling the flame for fear that the confession might go out. As for me, I didn't miss a scrap of this report, which radically changed the way I saw our world.

"...the shadowy presence had not left me, in the evening when I walked through the alleys of Copou Park in Iassy, waiting in vain for Mariuca to thank her for the poppies she painted in despair, in Budapest when I met with the writer Gyula Illyés on Rose Hill and he told me about the small hotel in front of Notre-Dame where he stayed in a newly liberated Paris; in Moscow near the Kaluzhskaya subway station when I was returning home late after listening to Richter. Was the shadow, too, wondering how the great pianist was able to get from the Petrov those sublime sounds, with his awkward fingers and his woodcutter's hands? In Sofia, when, tipsy, I would come out of the *mekhana*, he was there; I had learned to see with my entire body, I had eyes in my back, most importantly, never blink, the newcomers made fun of the old-timers with this oh-so-French smugness, until the day when they were caught. The little 'lecturer' posted in Stara Zagora, nominated 'foreign cooperation specialist' thanks to the intervention of his father, an ambassador, called me in the middle of the night: 'They're harassing me.' What did you do for them to persecute you that way? 'I gave *The Gulag Archipelago* to one of my colleagues.' Quick, go get it back and jump on the first train to Sofia. Not to mention engineered accidents and blackmailing attempts, but also warnings and trust building when the demon is disguised as, or turns into, a guardian angel. The long habit of being accompanied by an invisible presence one must constantly beware of, without showing any sign of alarm, became a second nature..."

A paranoiac, your young Frenchman, Vetrov! Who's rambling, Comrade, who's persecuting? P could not see me, but I was certain he knew I was sitting in the dark a few meters away from him and the teacher, whose precious testimonial about our police states' ways kept me wanting to hear more.

"...how good it feels when it's over, and it's over each time I go back to the West, as an ordinary tourist enjoying the sauna in Loma during a vacation in the heart of Finland, or savoring a hot chocolate at the Café Mozart in Vienna. Before you know it, though, the murky longing comes back with a revenge. Yes, it feels good when it stops, but it feels even better when it starts all over again, with the French teacher posted in Pskov, who wanders aimlessly in the hallway of the French embassy in Moscow, built of Armenian *tufa*; 'I'm being followed, day and night,' she complains, flanked by two attachés, arm in arm, walking her back to the plane, the teacher struggles, she doesn't want to leave. Me either. If he stopped eavesdropping on my conversations, if he were not filming me from his office window in the Ministry of Interior, located next to the embassy, it seems to me that I would be a mere shadow of my former self. This manhunt I try to elude gives meaning to my life, but how come I was never able to identify him with certainty?"

Enough, Vetrov! Is your vision so blurred that you did not notice your young Frenchman, the teacher who became cultural attaché, is neurotic?

The same is, was, and will be said of me too. Neurotic, this lover of freedom who is not afraid of throwing himself into the bear's jaws while trying to slip through the net set by the totalitarian state? Who is suffering from neurosis if not our camp as a whole? Paranoia of an entire continent, a complex of encirclement that takes over an entire nation and leads to the worst madness.

P had let the fire die. The two men were silent. It was dark. I could no longer see them. "Russian silence, the old inclination toward Potemkin villages, smoke screens, the occult, the mystical.

Vast white silence. Evil charm of secret. Heavy secrets burden the secret-keeper, isolate him from his fellow men; who discovers someone else's secret holds him in his power. Intimidation, destabilization are the means to be admitted into the other's privacy, taking from him what he values the most. The agent artfully plays on the keyboard of fear."

P got up and, as he was heading back to the villa, delivered those remarks in an incantatory tone but with a touch of irony in his voice.

Now you're mesmerized, Vetrov, hypnotized, in thrall to the power of suggestion by a master of manipulation, you no longer control your behavior, you're going to toe the line, not even being aware of it, you'll end up in a position of complete dependency.

What if it was the other way around? All P and his friend did was open my eyes. And now that the scales have fallen, I am determined to not close my eyes ever again.

It's not us but yourself that you're trying to convince of the legitimacy of your reversal; you're getting confused, Vetrov.

Even though this lengthy effort at remembering, this slow anamnesis, left me exhausted, it also lightened my burden, a sweet fatigue, I feel as if I've grown wings and, at last, I fly away as I fall asleep. Is this what they call the sleep of the Just? *It's high time we remind you of the crimes you're guilty of, Vetrov.*

When I woke up, I saw a parcel placed in full view on the small table of the cell, an ordinary grocery bag in which had been placed, not wrapped in anything, *the meat hook, do you recognize it, Vetrov?*

How could I not recognize it? I had thought I could chase away the nightmare, Vladik had spent hours cleaning the blood stains on the car's front seat; I had thought I could banish forever the vision of Ludmila's face twisted by pain, the open wounds, the blood gushing with each thrust, I would have liked to end my life then, *you should have terminated the murderer you had become.*

The warder is now waking up too. Falling asleep didn't bother him, since he knew with certainty that I wouldn't attempt to escape or commit suicide. Escape is impossible without an intervention orchestrated from the outside, and I must admit I love life way too much to want to put an end to it. The warder yawns, shakes himself, walks to the end of the corridor, goes into raptures, *everything has disappeared under an immense white mantle.*

Is it a gift from Heaven? Is it grandmother who dispatched from on high those thousands of white-winged angels over Moscow? So, the tales from the image box don't all end badly after all. Grandmother's angels swaddle the petrified city in their blankets. The festive snow is greeting me, ephemeral yet lasting, evanescent yet substantial. It is a melodious and melancholy song, a sentimental ballad of olden days performed by angels on the snow violin. Desirable snow, talking snow, dancing, singing, floating, crawling and flying snow, I am not alone since the snow is falling, reminiscent of a fresh-blown flower, similar to budding love; snow is what is left after one has lost everything. I like the snow that never melts, but I also like the snow that turns pale and dies without a word, and I must admit I experience a murky pleasure at feasting my eyes on impure snows, yellowish soup loaded with all of our waste, accursed and wicked snow, cruel snow, the burial snow of millions of poor souls!

Everything has disappeared under an immense white mantle, the fact that a guy like the warder with his drunkard's mug is still able to wonder like a child speaks volumes about our people's contradictions. *Soon the only trace left of you will be some yellow urine in the snow.* Soon I'll emerge from the rubble and will reach the golden mountain.

Russian balancing act, ambivalence: the immaculate mantle is also a shroud and, as if I could forget, the shouts, the insults, the noise of the heavy keys turning in locks that I'll never get used to, would bring me back to my grim condition. Splash, splash, the overpowering lapping noise of water in one of my neighbors' cell. No sooner has he left than it is necessary to make a clean sweep. *Yet another traitor who's going to end up in the slaughterhouse*, mutters the old hag, shuffling along the corridor.

And again, the freeze after the thaw, the cold after the warm, and the hope of pardon fading away.

You shouldn't have returned to Moscow, comrade Vetrov. The warder made the remark matter-of-factly. Criticism or compassion? It was not my destiny to flee. *This was not the destiny they had in mind for you.* Am I as spineless as you say? *In Paris you thought you could become a free electron.* It didn't happen overnight. Like those subterranean rivers digging their beds for a long time before reaching the surface and flowing freely in the open, the impressions left by the evening in Meudon were first suppressed by the hectic activity of my life, my cover as a commercial attaché as demanding as my spy job. However, instead of hardening as useless concretions, those impressions continued to live in me, branching out, spreading, getting around pockets of resistance, absorbing others, *until they submerged you entirely, Vetrov! Now here is a nice self-criticism, Comrade, all is not lost then!*

I'm past the self-criticism stage, such an exercise belongs to my previous life, it's the other Vetrov who was invited to go through it, *the old Vetrov, the one who will soon be reduced to mortal remains*, the one whose name will be dragged through the mud, the one who will be called all the names under the sun, accused of all the evils in the world, villainy, perfidy, desertion, felony, defection, abandonment, corruption, I am just repeating the litany of your accusations, *Vetrov the deceitful, the hypocrite, the traitor, you are guilty of high treason, your life hangs by a thread!*

What if those ramifications, those underground deployments were trying to work their way into the very depths of our country? *And if the proponents of a more open relationship with the West were to win over the proponents of a closed country, what sense would your refusal to cooperate make?* Russian volte-face, anything is possible in this country. *It's up to you to jump on this proof of our goodwill!* It's up to me to take this new role, to lend myself to this new game if I want to get out of this dump. *Out with it, Vetrov, confess, the Praga is not far!* All right then, if that's what you want to know, yes, I did go back to Meudon, I have nothing left to hide anymore. Once you've tasted the forbidden fruit, the temptation is great to have another bite. Yes, I went to the pink villa again, months later, for Midsummer's Day.

On the terrace in the park, the evening had begun with a reading of Denis Fonvizin's work. I was struck by the purity of the language and by the contemporary relevance of the topics addressed by Russia's first writer. The foreign students' diction was flawless: who was behind this exercise? I could not help seeing some secret intention in this public reading.

"Poor Ivanushka, being Russian is an ineffaceable flaw. Mother, when you talk about things Russian, I would like to be a hundred thousand French miles away." Shame and pride of being Russian. In *The Brigadier*, Fonvizin overtly mocked the Russians' strong liking for French ways. "The Gentlemen-travelers are lying when depicting France as Paradise on earth." The audience had brought the house down before breaking up and dispersing through the park. What was the meaning of such applause? Was I the only Francophile among the Russians present at this performance? And why did the French members of the audience approve so easily of Fonvizin's play, the intention of which was to denigrate French manners?

As I was wondering if I was not myself, two centuries later, a character from The Brigadier deserving Fonvizin's mockery, an affable middle-aged woman, all excited to learn I was a representative of the Soviet trade mission, had come up to me with her glass in one hand. "The whole world would be American if it weren't for the cradle of socialism!" After her sensational statement, the woman bragged about having picked up a cigarette butt on the lawn of our embassy. "It is prohibited," she had added, thinking I'd be flattered, "to litter the soil of the workers' country." Which one of us was the most ridiculous? This middle-class woman who idolized us and took a perverse delight in sawing the branch on which she was sitting *or the Soviet agent mesmerized by the suave French manners?*

I was not seduced by their manners, but by the degree of freedom they enjoyed, exchanging opposing opinions at no risk to anyone.

Before they had time to reach the other end of the park, guests and students mingled, and discussions were lively under the cedar tree. I was glad to see it again as if meeting an old friend. Diehard optimists believed both systems could find a point of convergence. In the émigrés' corner, there was a lot of moaning over Russia's misfortune, the occidentalists were bickering with the slavophiles, Lenin was compared to Robespierre, the Russian Revolution to the French Revolution; for some, Communism was just an avatar of Russian despotism, for others, it was a monstrous outgrowth of western thinking.

"The most serious flaw of democracy is that any citizen can get involved in anything. Here, everyone parades around, flaunting oneself, making a spectacle of oneself!" What kind of game was the bourgeois who was tracking me playing, expecting me to back up her statements? Who was showing off, flaunting oneself, making a spectacle of oneself if not her and her kind? If she was trying to make me decry the country of human rights, the maneuver had failed. I confess, I suddenly felt the urge to shut her up, when Father Kolya grabbed me by the arm and took me aside, inviting me to come visit their library.

A genuine treasure. Talk, Vetrov, lift the veil, you have nothing to lose. All the books banned by Soviet censorship were there on the shelves. While in KGB training, I had been allowed to read the most famous ones, Kravchenko, Amalrik, Grossman, and of course the Archipelago; there is no way I could not have known about writers being imprisoned, exiled or locked up in psychiatric hospitals. Even though I didn't take part directly in this repression, I was a member of the Service that implemented it, and thought that certain books had to be banned because they were minefields aimed at blowing up the system. *Yet, the attraction was the strongest, tell us Vetrov!*

Kolya told me at length about the samizdats from Central and Eastern Europe which had escaped our attention, speaking volumes about the slow but real decay of the regime, undermined as it was by the termites of this muted resistance. Manuscripts circulated clandestinely, readers clung to them as if a lifeline.

The Spider Web Mask, How I will be Hung, Love and Garbage, New Attempt at Sending a Booby-Trapped Parcel, The Prisoner's Long Journey, Zbigniew Morsztyn Comes Back to Warsaw From Königsberg, The Pencil's Dream, Comrade Münchhausen, and other texts already written or still to be written. Take notice, Comrades, mighty oaks from little acorns grow. You won't be able to contain the floodtide, so many short texts traveling through obscure channels from East to West, and coming back to their starting point, so many tiny windows allowing the escape from suffocation, so many oases to regain strength.

A tiny window through which to escape, that's what you badly need where you're currently rotting, Vetrov. It's my turn to be the spider web mask's victim, *it's your turn to be trapped and live the prisoner's long journey,* my turn to feel light at the bottom of the dungeon and be able to laugh at this huge farce, Comrade Münchhausen!

What do you have to say about all this, little roach? I'm about to look very much like you. I, too, am an insect with an incomplete metamorphosis, even if I have neither membranous back wings nor semi-rigid front wings. Like you, little *blatta orientalis,* I cannot fly away, *however great your desire to be with your loved ones again,* however great my desire to see again the friend with the prudence of a snake and infinite attention to details, *open your heart, Vetrov, unburden your conscience,* why would I hide anything, I met him only once in Meudon, during that unforgettable night, *during which he had done everything he could to make you aware he had noticed you while pretending otherwise.* How skillfully he made himself scarce, turning his back at the right moment, pretending to go in the direction opposite to where he wanted to go, *you were not wary enough, Vetrov,* quite the contrary, I was right to be trusting, on both sides men aspire to extend the hand of friendship to one another, *the rot has already set in,* clouds of insects are working at breaking down the Wall, the wind of History is rising, the Jericho trumpets will soon be heard!

All this sounds too good to be true, Vetrov, no one ever saw the muzhik fly away on a red rooster and land on the Eiffel Tower, no one ever saw the poor shepherd marry the Tsar's daughter, no one ever saw the intrepid soldier come out of the petrified city, this is just a bunch of cock-and-bull stories, alright, Comrade, let's say I lapsed into second childhood, let's say I started believing in a friendship you declared impossible between two enemies, *impossible is the correct word, Vetrov, your so-called friend is just a keen sleuth, an intelligence professional,* an occasional counter-spy, a patriot who could not stand seeing the Soviet rats stick their teeth into his French cheese, *your friend deceived you like a rookie, Vetrov, Fonvizin's brigadier,* he had nothing to do with it, *you were totally hoodwinked, the skit was just an excuse, an appetizer before the main entrée, the conditioning, you had it coming to you, Vetrov, you would soon eat from your Frenchman's hand.*

In the corridor, someone clears his throat and spits on the floor. A long, oppressive silence follows. I no longer know where I stand, with their relentless rehashing of my biography I could end up believing them if they don't stop this charade. I forgot who I am, it's been a long time since I saw my face last, they took away the small broken mirror from my cell. Are they afraid I might slit my wrists? Then why did they leave the meat hook? They must be unsure of the way to handle me. Vetrov escapes them the same way he is escaping me. Time trickles like sand through my fingers, flying; since they took my watch from me, I lost track of the day and the time, my head is buzzing with scrambled, overlapping episodes of my life, *you'll soon be just a ridiculous puppet gesticulating in its cage,* torn between the burden of reminiscing and the longing for a new life.

There is no new life for wrecks of your kind.

Patience, Vetrov, patience, don't give up now, continue collecting, gathering and sticking together the shards of your memories. Sitting on the edge of your well, keep pulling the bucket up, relentlessly, until the last second, inch by inch. It would be illusory to attempt to block exits. Millions of people are waiting in the darkness without breathing a word, and this wait has the power of a magnet.

You belong to this land, Vetrov, you grew up with the legends of our people, in your own way you are heralding the big night and a brighter future, yesterday's enemies will embrace, choirs will form, flowers will be thrown from both sides of the Wall, *you play the prophet, Vetrov, the people cannot be fooled, the Russians know when they're dealing with impostors,* you have eyes but you can't see the new world about to be born, *thanks to Comrade Vetrov, thanks to his insane action,* there is no need to ridicule me, *we are materialists and atheists, we don't believe in miracles, Comrade,* and yet a true miracle is in the making, which will reunite what was separated, restore yesteryear's relations, this is what is achieved by transmission, *treason, Vetrov,* accomplished by a single man positioned at the right place at the right time.

Lovely story, Vetrov, but who will believe you? And what would grandmother say if she could see her intrepid soldier bound hand and foot with a velvet ribbon? Certainly the French are not the brutes we are, Vetrov, they wouldn't have shackled you, but they nevertheless didn't let go of you after they got you out of a tight spot by repairing the black Peugeot.

During that summer of nineteen seventy-five, after the incident in Montreal, as I waited in Moscow for Svetlana's return, a month later than mine, I was brooding over my grievances, wanting to think only about myself, *you would have liked to flee, go back to the West, we considered sending you to Marseille as a Consul, but the French, your dear friends,* denied me the necessary authorization for my posting, a retaliatory measure for the recruiting I performed in Paris, *unless it was to put you off the track,* they owed me nothing, I have nothing to blame them for, *yet Monsieur Vetrov was moping, Monsieur Vetrov, the spoiled child from Paris, was not satisfied with the job the Party offered him,* in charge of relations with capitalistic countries for the Ministry of Foreign Trade, *Monsieur Vetrov pouted,* and here I was, nominated to a job in Yasenevo, the KGB's brand-new headquarters, *which you first viewed as a golden closet* where I would be stuck for good, *you won't leave the Soviet Union ever again, you're condemned to vegetate in an office,* but what an office! To me, lieutenant colonel Vetrov, were flooding all the reports from our residents posted all over the world! A strategic position from which I could see better than anyone else how Russia was descending into the abyss, I witnessed the progressive paralysis of vital centers, I observed that the waste inside and the pillage outside resolved nothing, I denounced loud and clear the corruption of our elites who cared only about their immediate personal interests, *you suggested to your superiors a comprehensive overhaul of structures and methods for scientific and technical intelligence gathering*, a first step before proposing an in-depth reform of Soviet society as a whole, *your proposal went unheeded*, it was only then that I began despairing of my situation, *you took to drinking, Vetrov, while Svetlana lived in style*, this was not about a personal crisis but about a bankrupt world view and the superpower that embodied it, *it was all about you, Vetrov, you were deteriorating*, Svetlana sensed it, she wanted to slow down my fall, *it was her*, it was always her, *who took you to Kresty.*

Happiness was right there, Vetrov, within reach, by the old willows reflecting in the Tvertsa, in the blueness of the flax fields, a simple happiness, *a Russian dacha*, the vast garden, the pink apple-trees in the orchard, Katya's cottage cheese, the lovely stories told by Maria who had served as a maid in Alexis Tolstoy's home, *and the fishing from the banks of the Tversa*, and mushroom gathering with friends, *the warmth from the Russian stove*, grandmother's ancient icon restored by Svetlana, *sweet Russia*, Russian dream, *blue Russia you weren't able to keep, Vetrov*, that's right, I was unable to keep you, matushka, I was unable to keep you my little fox, and you either, my sweet Vladik, I kiss your hands, Svetik my darling, and your eyes; and you, my son, my pride, I send you my love, may you both grant me your pardon! *Let's hope you'll see both of them again*, may I see you again and, please God, spend the rest of my life making you forget the harm I've done!

How could they forget, Vetrov, you have a short memory, what do you make of the meat hook? How to forget the bloodshed, the streams of blood, the immense rivers of blood; one evening grandmother, as if upset and with a heavy heart, told me how activists in leather coats had stormed the farm, knocked over the kasha to the ground, spat on the icons and broken them, trampled them underfoot, had grabbed the boots, undressed the master, and whipped him naked in the yard before throwing his body down the well. In order to be happy under the old willows, you had to be able to not think, listen, or speak and to slowly regress to the blue cocoon of a legendary Russia.

Instead, Vetrov, you lost interest in the blue flax fields, in the pink apple trees of the dacha in Kresty, Vetrov drifting away, *Russia is not the sick one, it is you, the pathetic hero of a pitiful story,* Vetrov going downhill, drinking his nights away, *while Svetlana, who had grown tired of it all, cheated on you,* I forgive you sweetheart, *how distressing it was to watch Comrade Vetrov go downhill,* I was about to execute a somersault, *that's putting it mildly, a tumble not to boast about, a miserable adventure that ended poorly,* how could I disagree with you, Ludmila has nothing to do with it, I am the only one who has to pay for it, I'll show them who this Vetrov they underestimated for so long is, I'll show them what he's made of! At the far end of the corridor, a door is opened then slammed with a hellish noise. "Lena!" cried the prisoner who will say no more. Someone slid an envelope under my door. There is a picture inside, Svetlana looks radiant among the budding willows by the Tvertsa. The cockroach remains transfixed on my knee. A ribbon of fresh snow borders the window. My hands are shaking suddenly, a trembling which seems to come from somewhere else takes over my body, penetrates me, assaults me, goes right through me, innervating my body, I feel like shouting for joy, but no sound comes out of my throat. My body is being covered with rough woody patches, tender green young leaves grow from me. I am a tree reflecting in the Tvertsa's peaceful waters. Did I come back to hear the ring of the Russian spring bells?

You shouldn't have returned to Moscow, Vetrov. I shouldn't have but I decided to come back ten years ago and I won't leave again. *You're not a tree, Vetrov, you're a cockroach, you thrive on garbage, you feed yourself on rubbish.* During all those years, I was like a cockroach indeed, going in circles with the feeling that nothing had changed, that there was no future, that the present was a mere repetition of the past. *The bottleneck is getting narrower.* Back to the Center, days are all alike, hours are spent reading operation reports, going through scientific journals, writing summaries to the attention of superiors who would not read them. *Back to the base, back to the basics.* Like the others during all those years I had to swim in this gruel. They have lost their taste for life, their eyes are vacant, interchangeable masks were substitutes for their individual faces, lives going to the dogs, twigs floating in the wind; they end up being all alike, silhouettes losing one after the other the fourth and then the third dimensions. Like others, I am bogged down in the tepid mess, I feel my heart contract and shrivel. Neither dog nor wolf, say the French, neither fish nor meat say the Russians. I have the feeling of sliding down a muddy slope with nothing to grab hold of to stop my fall. *That's where petty bourgeois individualism led you, Vetrov.* I could not imagine myself rotting at a desk job, even within the glamorous Directorate T in charge of scientific and technical intelligence; *those who have known the wan light of dawn and evasive glances cannot put them out of mind.* I could not and will never be able to put them out of my mind, but I became aware of the existence of a Soviet time. This country which was mine had claimed for itself the sad power of freezing time. Nothing had moved. The present continued to copy the past. The dream had definitely turned into a nightmare and the nightmare was our reality. And I could no longer accept it.

The pink villa syndrome, Vetrov, but despite your struggling, you are still attached to Russia and she to you, with its grey housing blocks, its courtyards filled with rubbish, its peeling façades, its puffing tramways, its stench of sour cabbage, with that fear coating everything, with the haggard looks, sticky eyes, nodding heads, excruciating silence, endless waiting lines, *endless winters,* and those useless cranes with their arms lifted toward the sky, yes, this is the country I'm attached to and missed when I was in Paris and Montreal, *and it was with a malicious pleasure that you reconnected with suspicion, funny business,* and the art of omission, and extreme feelings, *and this familiar je ne sais quoi in people interactions you missed abroad*, the two faces of Russia, a country of wanderers, *whatever you do, Vetrov, try as you may to mimic the French, you'll never become a petit-bourgeois, you belong to this land*, yes, but not in the way you understand it, *you did everything you could to escape from Mother Russia*, but I came back and threw myself into her arms, *beg her absolution, kiss her feet, sing, sing, Vetrov*, yes I sing loud enough to shake the prison walls, loud enough to be heard by the people from as far as the Red Square, Lake Baikal, Vladivostok!

The noise of gates, the grinding of keys in the lock. Has the time come? No, it's just the old hag grumbling as she delivers a package to the warder. *Here is a knife for you, Vetrov, from your friends.* What game are you playing, what's the point of this dubious act? Is this a new invitation to suicide? Or do you want me to hurl myself at the warder? *Made in France, Vetrov. It's true, your friend did not forget you, Vetrov*, all I need is to know that he still thinks about me. *Do they believe they could exfiltrate you without our help?* By returning to Moscow, I made the decision to throw myself into the bear's jaws; I wouldn't be true to myself if I accepted your offer. *You won't let a treason stop you, Vetrov, you're addicted to double games!*

You're wrong, all I have done since I came back to Moscow has been simple, no more duplicity, I have acted in agreement with my thinking, *with your handling officer's thinking, Vetrov, you became his puppet in the spring of 1981*, it's the other way around, on that day I decided to cast off my chains, to break off with fate. *Fatal drift*, a drift which is not mine, it is an entire society adrift, decaying, bogged down, debacle, the boat is sinking, no more beacon, no more star, no more golden age, sneaky fear numbing a whole people, a lead weight choking creativity, scientists under house arrest, no longer able to innovate. *That's when Comrade Vetrov enters the scene as the savior of the Motherland?* You can mock me, Comrades, but don't you see we were rushing headlong into disaster? Resources were wasted everywhere, money was spent left and right for information gathering, for copying others' inventions with mixed results, whichever the field of activity, we glaringly failed. Where are the days when Soviet scientists were building the gyrotron, sputnik, the annular radiotelescope? *So then you decided to jump into the abyss?* For the return of hope, for Russia's rebirth! *Your French friends gave you an English name, which did not bother you in the least!* Farewell, a premonitory name, fasten your belts, Comrades, you have no idea of the conflagration awaiting you! *Farewell Mister Vetrov, it's true that we've been rather stupid not to realize immediately what game you were playing, we thought you were an ordinary murderer, the letters you wrote to your wife from Siberia got us thinking, but to say we were impressed by your boasting, not by a long shot!*

The cockroach had fled to the window and stopped on the ribbon of snow, putting distance between us so I can see it better; it's going about its business from one world to the other, it is little worried by the margins and limits set by men, it's doing as it pleases, only following its instinct. Which one enjoys the most freedom in this city, in this empire? The blatta orientalis or the homo sovieticus? *You're either with us, or against us.* "You're either with us, or against us," I don't want to have to choose between sides anymore, before being a Soviet man, I am a human being!

You're a man, Vetrov, a father, a husband, a lover, a man with a pounding heart, a heart driven crazy by the Spring!

It was warmer, and snowdrops were blooming in the suburban underbrush. I had been champing at the bit for too long, *you were burning to get back into the game, Vetrov, you sent a Paris engineer a postcard mailed in Hungary by a relative.* I took an insane risk. *"I need to see you," five words written in a feverish handwriting, a laconic message that said a great deal about your frame of mind.* A bottle at sea that could have been intercepted by anyone, a Hungarian civil servant, a French post office employee, a nosy neighbor. I was counting on Jacques, *your friend the engineer,* to serve as an intermediary with our enemies. And what if he panicked? What if he were to speak nonsense to those who would interrogate him about the source of the postcard, about the sender, about the meaning of the message? I hadn't seen him in seven long years! We certainly feasted together, *and he paid for the repair of the Peugeot you crashed single-handedly*, he could very well have forgotten all about me. Even assuming he decided to transmit my postcard to my French colleagues, *you already considered them your colleagues, Vetrov*, weren't they going to be suspicious, believe it was a ploy and drop me? *You got it right, Vetrov, your card was left unanswered, French politeness is no longer what it used to be, your dear friends didn't trust you, they thought you were a lure, a bait.*

Three or four months went by, I was fretting. Did Jacques receive my S.O.S., did he inform the French Services? What if he gave my card to our resident in Paris? I would have been in a right fix. Talk about a state of commotion in my head by the end of the year nineteen-eighty! It's one thing to decide to cross the Rubicon; it's another to reach the other side, *to deal the mortal blow to the Soviet monster. That's what you were boasting about, Vetrov, during one of your drinking binges!* I'm not the only one who thinks that it's high time for the country to right itself, *things are changing in the Party, at least in the remote provinces*, the name of a certain Yeltsin from Sverdlovsk is being rumored in the corridors of the Service. Yet I made sure not to show my opinions, a tough school, dreadful solitude, *and Svetlana who did not speak to you anymore*, never had New Year's Eve been so gloomy. *You cast off, Vetrov.* Breaking with those I love, was it a requisite for action?

I couldn't take the waiting any more. In February nineteen eighty-one an electronics trade show was organized at the Armand Hammer Center by the Ministry of Foreign Trade. It was natural for me to attend, and I knew for certain I could meet the Schlumberger representative, *an expert in electronics you had met in Paris*, I risked my all and asked him to deliver a new letter to Jacques. *It was a matter of life or death.* That's precisely what I wrote in my message to Jacques. *A bunch of amateurs, your Frenchmen, Vetrov, and airy at that, they did not even bother to answer your card, yet you were set on selling your soul to those guys!* I still believed in Jacques's friendship, he had got me out of trouble. *You lost your legendary intuition, Vetrov, you rub shoulders with smooth talkers unable to keep their promises.* Jacques did not let me down. *He eventually answered you.* He dispatched his collaborator, a scientist who had invented the Myosotis teleprinter, an intelligent, courteous and helpful man, *a naive man who could have ruined your dark machination.* Xavier was not that naive since he took the precaution to call me from a public phone booth! *Elementary, Vetrov!* Maybe so, but I could breathe again, the contact had been established; moreover this Xavier was a well-mannered Frenchman as I like them, *the flower of bourgeoisie*, a man a hundred miles away from our sordid world, an aristocrat!

You ran a huge risk by meeting your baron that day, the fourth of March, 1981, in front of the Beriozka store. "The idea that the world is not as we see it or as we believe it to be, that invisible forces lead it, is shared by the agent and the monk alike." This statement, uttered by P addressing his interlocutor of that one evening, came to my mind during this first contact. *The pink villa syndrome, Vetrov, you were ready to let the angel from Paris lead you!* Xavier thought I wanted to defect and assured me that France was willing to offer me political asylum. *They had not understood that you no longer wanted to leave Russia, Vetrov.*

How to explain to Xavier that I had decided to play Russian roulette? Xavier thought I was taking him for a ride, he wanted proof, *you promised to provide evidence*, he was amused, *"it's like being in a detective movie," he said*, and the location chosen for the first operational rendezvous reinforced his feeling. "Why the Borodino Battle Museum?" he wondered. He saw an intention in such a choice which he found titillating. For the French, this name is associated with a battle won by Napoleon, but we consider that this battle was won by the Russian army. My reasons were more mundane. Svetlana was still working at the Museum part time. I often waited for her there and no one would have found it odd to see me sitting in the Lada at the corner of the pocket park behind the Panorama, *the pocket park that became the strategic point of lieutenant colonel Vetrov's brilliant operation.*

That's where I revealed to Xavier the names of the two

Frenchmen I had recruited in Paris, *and who were still collaborating with us*; as evidence of my willingness to cooperate, I gave him a complete organization chart of our service. *A poorly rewarded gift, Vetrov, they are misers, those French!* Quite the contrary, persisting in believing I wanted to defect, they offered me the passport. I turned it down, Comrades. *Self-sacrificing Vetrov, Vetrov playing the scapegoat, and now you think you're Jesus Christ!*

I had enough. *For ten years you'd been brooding on your revenge, wrongly believing that you had not been taken seriously and that your services had not been rewarded properly.* The moment I had dreamt of so intensely had come. The link was restored. I was breathing again, I found a renewed pleasure in going to the office, I was zealous, spending nights working. *Your Xavier was hooked*, he forwarded a two-hundred-page file about the methods used by our scientific intelligence experts, rendezvous followed rendezvous, Xavier Xeroxed non-stop, with his wife Claude's help, the pump was primed, the Paris "cousins" eventually received a fifteen-hundred-page file, *the Smirnov dossier*, including among other things the complete list of the officers in charge of scientific data gathering, *the documents did not transit through the embassy*, Xavier did not trust diplomats, I didn't either, but he assured me the liaison had been established, I didn't doubt his word, *yet you were worried, Vetrov, and rightly so*, yes I feared that the baron's lack of experience in intelligence affairs could lead him to commit an irreparable mistake, *your French friend was on the same wavelength as you, he knew that despite his immense goodwill, Xavier was not incapable of a faux pas.*

And I know my time is precious even if I believe in my lucky star. After all, I'm the son of Corporal Ippolit Vasilevich Vetrov, who was drafted from the onset of the German attack in June, 1941, and who was among the very few survivors to parade on Red Square in 1945! *And so, you became a member of the pink villa network, Vetrov.* Did P guess that I constantly thought about him throughout this phase? *They studied Gurdjieff's teachings, they were ahead in their research on telepathy. They are the ones, he is the one, rather, who conditioned you, focusing his attention on your subconscious, submitted you to his influence and triggered the fateful impulsion on the day set by his superior.* If you say so, Comrades! But you forget to mention the detail that changes everything. Things happened the way they did because I wanted it, and I myself had used a telepathy channel to call for help to the one I dreamt of becoming a partner with.

The roach's elytra are quivering. Fright or jubilation? It's huddling down in my navel. What do we know about the power of dictyoptera's sensitive bristles? They're thought to have tactile and also olfactory and auditory functions. Why not telepathic? The roach is my guardian angel sent by grandmother. I have nothing to fear any more.

You have nothing left to fear, Vetrov, your fedora is battered, your trench coat from Tati's is frayed, you can keep your collar up as much as you want, you scare nobody. You're just a walk-on, an airport novel character, your entire story is a blatant lie, you fooled no one, you've been duped, you're the victim of your megalomania, you ridiculed us, that's why you must keep out of the limelight, and we are going to do everything to ensure it stays that way. I'm going to disappear, I resigned myself to it. *There are many ways to make you disappear, think about the car waiting in front of the Praga, remember the gift from your friends!*

But why the knife, why the meat hook if it's not to invite me to end my life? The trap is too crude for me to fall into it. I can't imagine them trying to make me commit another crime. Such an approach wouldn't be that subtle either. No, I have no intention to rush at the bitch, even less at the warder, it wouldn't be long before they'd grab me and make me see reason. True, such a gesture on my part would confirm their diagnosis. *Vladimir Ippolitovich Vetrov, an antisocial, dangerous, uncontrollable element.* So what are they trying to convey to me given the fact they know I am not going to fall in with their blatant guile? They still view me as a sensualist, a *bon viveur*, first of all they think I would be more of a threat dead than alive. *Don't get carried away Vetrov, already claiming martyrdom, the Paris enfant terrible that you were became an ordinary troublemaker,* a burdensome agent provocateur we would rather have others take care of instead of keeping him at home, *an opportunity not to be missed, Vetrov, remember the blue roses, the white shirt, the burgundy tie!* How lovingly did Svetlana prepare them, and for what kind of departure? *It would not be your first turnaround, Vetrov!*

Svetlana and I enjoyed running, climbing up trees where we spent hours telling one another about our childhoods. Svetik was a fast learner; in elementary school she had memorized her lessons like millions of Soviet kids. Up in our trees, we liked reciting together the refrains of those years. The Reds will crush the Whites to the last one… Collectivization is advancing full steam through the marshes…Soviet science reroutes rivers… Later, while shopping in Paris, Svetlana remembered the slogan and completed it: Soviet science can conquer space but is unable to provide housewives with a washing machine or a pressure cooker. Up in the trees, where I enjoyed building a precarious dwelling, it was like sitting on a cloud. Svetlana would bring homemade pirozhki, and we would bite into the stuffed buns with ravenous appetite. Then we would resume reciting our lessons. Communism is the Soviet power plus electrification of the whole country…Let's protect our country with the utmost vigilance… Russian elephants are the happiest elephants on earth…The Soviet people won the Great Patriotic War… Soviet thieves are the most honest thieves in the whole world! Humorous anecdotes were spreading at the same pace as slogans, but it was only in our tree, away from eavesdroppers, that the young students we were could freely mix criticism and praise. Once, during one of those above-ground musings, we wondered about the shortcuts, if not the vast blanks, in our history manual. What happened exactly between August 1939 and June 1941? "What do you think Volodia, darling," Svetlana had asked me some other time, "of our hero Pavlik Morozov who denounced his father to the authorities as a social-traitor?" Cowardly, I hadn't answered. Frankly speaking, the black holes of Soviet history did not bother us that much. We had better things to do. Between two kisses, we were more concerned by our personal story and our families'. Like my mother, Svetlana's father was born in a village in the Volga region. His love for books had earned him the nickname of Turgenev. He, too, like grandmother, thought that the image box was full of stories which ended poorly.

How many times did grandmother tell me the tale of the Bladder, the Straw and the Shoe! "Once upon a time, there was a bladder, a blade of straw and a shoe"... Yes, tell me, grandma! Tell me where they all met! "Not far from here, on the edge of the forest, they decided to go and chop wood for the winter, and then they reached a river..." Was there a bridge, grandma, to cross the river? "No, there was no bridge!" How did they manage to cross the river? "We're going to climb on you," said the shoe to the bladder which didn't agree and suggested the blade of straw would stretch over the river to serve as a footbridge. Did the straw go along, grandma? "Alas, it did!" How does the story end, grandmother? "The shoe started walking on the blade of straw and broke it, falling into the water, carried away by the current." And the bladder, grandma? "It laughed, it laughed so much, it burst!" Svetlana knew the tale better than I. At school, she had spent a whole winter reading it, writing it, drawing it, singing it, playing it, dancing it. How I'd love to hear grandmother again, one day, telling me the story, how I'd like to see you dance it, my sweet ballerina, my beloved poppy! *Svetlana doesn't feel like dancing anymore, all she has left is her eyes to cry, Vetrov.* Don't cry, my little fox, I wish I could dry your tears, I'd like to go back to Kresty next spring, everything would be like in the good old days again. You'd blow your cheeks like the bladder, they'd turn all red until bursting...*pschtt*...you'd jump off the tree and I'd join you in the grass at the water's edge.

The big plunge, Volodia, you took it on Friday May 1, 1981. The encounter of my life. *You're forgetting Ludmila, Vetrov.* I forgot no one, neither my wife nor Ludmila, nor the two or three officers from the Service who secretly supported me. *We want names, Vetrov!* I forget neither my country nor the world balance, *come back to earth, Vetrov,* more beautiful than a romance, those secret rendezvous for months, and several times a month, in my car or at the market on Vavilova Street. *All that for crates of whisky bottles and for a coat made in Paris!* That's your way to look at it, you'll do everything you can to belittle me, *you're just an ordinary guy, Vetrov, driven by primitive impulses,* an ordinary man who decided, one day, to transcend himself, *a misfit who takes himself for a knight,* the more you charge me the more you contribute to my glory!

How can you believe, Vetrov, that this lanky guy, who let his hair grow in the spring in order not to look like what he is—a career soldier—could dupe us? You were fooled by his looks, his coarse and kindly appearance, his clumsy gait, his friendly and rustic manners, it did not cross your minds that, aware of his image, he could make use of it. You thought he was a *drifting military attaché,* you didn't see the atypical side of a man who had ceased to report to his hierarchy, sensing it was no longer reliable, *that's the version he gave you, Vetrov, your dear Paul could make you swallow any tall story.* I did not meet an agent but a man capable of sublimating himself in order to live what will remain for him the most beautiful period of his life, and mine! *You're turning lyrical, Vetrov, what a pity to see you singing an enemy's praises, as harmless as he may be.* If he were as harmless as you claim, you would not have harassed me the way you did about him. *You didn't tell us everything, Vetrov, you're probably keeping the best part for the end, confess, you still have some time left, today may not be the day yet.* Haven't I told you everything already, at great length? *Everything that crosses your mind amuses us, Vladimir Ippolitovich!* Don't mock, Comrades, the Vetrov case will soon be taught in counterintelligence schools! The scenario of the leak of the century will be described and explained by specialists, three thousand pages of archives stolen from the Soviet Service, this is no small deed, but what will capture the experts' attention in this affair is the resurgence of the human factor.

The human factor, there's the rub, Vetrov, this is your weak spot.

It's snowing again, the type of snow I like, frail, translucent, childhood snow, the same as the snow dancing outside the window in grandmother's izba.

The delivery of documents took only a few seconds. We spent the rest of the time exchanging points of view and getting better acquainted. With infinite patience, P listened to me, looked at me, was taking in the way I behaved, my way of being. He had noticed my need for understanding the true motives underlying the stated ones. He had understood that I was convinced, out of love for my country, that time had come to put an end to the totalitarian regime. We were fighting for the same ideal and in the same manner. One day, we attempted to isolate the inner workings that drive secret agents. Was it a trial they put themselves through deliberately for disturbing reasons rooted in childhood? Was it the need to get out of the rut, to not become a human wreck and to no longer be at the mercy of events? Beyond serving a cause which I viewed as just, wasn't I driven above all by the will to break down barriers and by the longing for transmutation? Subtle, the handling officer practiced maieutics. In his opinion, crossing over to the other side of the mirror implied the ability to play in both planes, being on both sides simultaneously. *Vetrov the pupil has fulfilled his Master's expectations.* I was given the opportunity to verify the soundness of his views. There is always a game within the game, and this can go very far. The one who thinks of himself as the manipulator is always more or less manipulated by the one he is supposed to manipulate. Willingly or not, any agent plays a double game. *Such theories should have made you more suspicious, Vetrov.* We only gradually unmasked ourselves. According to P, once you had tried that game, you could no longer live without it. Its theater is a mere parody even though the agent's playing techniques are similar to the comedian's. *Your officer is well-read, Vetrov.* Are there not different schools, different styles for agents as for actors, such as the Brechtian distanciation in acting, the followers of Diderot's Paradox of the Comedian, or Meyerbeer's and Stanislavski's students?

"This constant splitting of personality," I had asked P, "Could it lead to schizophrenia?" *Good question, Vetrov!* "On the contrary," he had answered me, "the awareness of the splitting, which implies a constant vigilance, facilitates the reconciling of the being's various components between which ordinary mortals are torn." "Isn't it driving this sharp focus on oneself and on the other to an extreme?" "Yes, indeed, and in the same motion. Your adversary lives with you, close and separate at the same time, he guesses your intentions, makes suggestions, tries to win you over, to reverse this energy, not against him but with him, so that the enemy becomes an ally?" *You've been used as a guinea-pig by your friend, Vetrov.*

If we were able to have those conversations at the height of the action, and in spite o f the constant tension weighting us down, it is because we both had decided to position ourselves outside and above the handling operation and to establish a relationship of trust between us.

You're getting ahead of yourself, Vetrov, Paul is just one of your associates, you're obsessed by him, seeing him everywhere, the agonizing anamnesis I'm engaged in doesn't care about chronology, *you're rewriting history, hoping naively that posterity will get interested in you,* I undertook to gather the broken pieces of the mirror, *you're bogged down in your fascination with your new master,* I am rebuilding myself by recollecting the meetings that followed, *you're skipping certain facts, you're focusing on others,* I am reappropriating my life, *you are what the Soviet State made you,* I refuse to be the mere product of an ideology I no longer share, *despite your recriminations, like it or not, it is the Soviet time which structures you,* a time which is frozen, *count on us to jog your memory,* count on me to evade your sway, *you're in our hands,* my body is in jail whereas my spirit is freeing itself from the burden of History, you desecrated the icon but you cannot extinguish the Mother's love for her child, you cannot shoot angels, nor the leaves nor the wind, I'm here at home in this cell as under the blue cedar tree, soon Moscow will have ceased to be a Soviet city. *Drunken ramblings, madman's talk.*

I wrap myself up in the blanket, outside it's freezing hard. I haven't slept a wink all night. One of my neighbors kept screaming. You'd think he was being tortured. Early this morning, they dragged him outside. No shooting, but a muted blow, the kind that makes your blood run cold. I'd like to bury myself in sleep but it is impossible because of this death rattle buzzing in my head, mixing with the questions hammered and rehashed for months by judges, investigators and other inquisitors, and with the answers I was hanging on to survive.

Put yourself in our shoes, Vetrov, if there is a risk that gangrene will spread to the whole body, shouldn't the rotten limb be cut off? Don't you think your grandmother would agree with us? Cut it off, if that makes you happy, I fear nothing now, I'm already gone, *you're no longer one of us, that's for sure,* I cast off but, like it or not, there's nothing you can do against the tidal wave which is about to sweep aside all that lies in its path, *here you are again with your prophecies, Vetrov,* I am no mystic, but it happens, it happened in Russian history, that an ordinary man receives the gift of clairvoyance, I tell you, soon darkness will dissipate, *stop your pompous stance, come back to earth, Vetrov, remember the softness of the grass under the willows lining the Tversa, unburden, the fault is grave but your confession is worth its weight in gold, it's up to you to become a free man again.*

P proceeded gradually, moving from the general to the particular. Even when about our trade, our conversations in the car always addressed the human component determining the agent's behavior. "Reading a voice, deciphering a look, sensing in one's inmost being the waves radiating from the other, enticing him if he is worth it, and building up a friendship with him. On the other hand, if dealing with a mediocre individual, give him the impression he won the game and withdraw because there is no point in wasting your time at contemptible games." P had an accurate measure of the risks I was taking and of the pressure I was under. He didn't hesitate to remind me of the rules of elementary prudence. "Do not leave any paper in the waste basket, control what you say, anticipate your moves, watch out but never forget that suspicion breeds suspicion, there's nothing like natural behavior. Advice was provided with brotherly compassion, giving me the help I needed to carry out my task. In case things would go wrong, P had recommended resorting to what he called the lizard's tactics. "Distance yourself, break free and leave a nonessential part of yourself to the pursuer." Hence, according to him, the necessity for me to assume several carefully crafted characters. "Any agent is the result of a concerted construction of a character part. The ultimate is creating a lure, a fictitious agent born ex nihilo, or even more subtle, a fictitious story attributed to a real agent, with his agreement or covertly." P had understood very well why I refused to defect, and he was contemplating helping me in the elaboration of a character that might have allowed me to avoid what he called the unveiling. I could only see in this gesture a sign of friendship on his part. It was out of the question for me to sneak away or wiggle out, even if it meant draining my cup to the last dregs. It was the requirement for the final success of my undertaking. *Your wishes may be fully granted soon, Vetrov: the rendezvous you are longing for is near!*

What one dreads, it's not dying as such, it's leaving behind the untilled garden, the unrepaired car, the unfinished sun room; the myriad of things that hold us to life, the mimosa bouquet I'd like to offer Svetlana, the Georgian wine at the Aragvi restaurant, and the electric model-train I'd promised Vladik.

A fictitious agent made up from scratch, a lure that we would have invented entirely, Vetrov? What if your friend was right? What if this entire story had just been a montage? What if this mountain of documents passed to the enemy comprised only fakes carefully forged by one of your colleagues? Had I defected to the West, you could have given substance to this theory. If you thought I was a mere fraud, you would not have thrown me in jail!

Paul and I often pretended all this was just a huge joke. "A Russian is ready to do anything if invited to go mushroom hunting," I had told him one day; without taking me at my word exactly, he had brought me marinated cèpes which we savored in the Lada. Of course we both knew that our days together were numbered but we almost never talked about it. "Secrets always end up seeping out," he had nonetheless told me once in a joking tone, and on that day we had touched on the idea of spending our old age in a dacha among birch trees by a pond, waiting for fish to rise to the bait with a few bottles in the cooler for the evening. P liked Russia, *a strange way to like us,* he appreciated our way of life, not only had he learned the Russian language, delighted by its harsh and deep tones, but he also never missed an opportunity to see the country, to visit the provinces if granted the authorization to travel. A conscientious agent who preferred meeting with young French teachers scattered throughout the Soviet Union, with a hands-on experience of Soviet life, over diplomatic dinners leading nowhere. He was careful not to jeopardize the teachers' position. All these small pieces of information that he was gathering he shared with me, not so much to verify their authenticity as to consolidate our friendship, surprising me and corroborating my own analysis.

"Hubbub. Men's raucous shouting, women's sharp shrieking. Smells of sweat, cabbage, cheap perfume, poorly refined gasoline, brine, mildew, mustiness, jostling again. Controlled and prohibited, always. And always complete chaos. Shambles in a straitjacket." P paid great attention to these atmosphere notes. "The room is tiny," the lecturer wrote, "the toilets are in despicable repair. One cannot live with two toddlers in this cubbyhole. I want to call my wife from the *obschezhitie* to alert her. You can't call abroad, not even to sister countries. We rush to the main post office on Gorki Street where is the only international telephone in Moscow. Before calling, you first need to give the duration of the conversation and pay in advance. They don't trust the deserving masses, foreigners even less." The lecturer had touched a raw nerve, this pathological distrust numbs the social body. Was he the young teacher I had heard confide to P that evening in Saint-Georges?

Spit out your anti-Soviet venom, Vetrov, as matters stand now, you're not exposing yourself to more risk! During one of our meetings in my Lada, *the blue Lada,* I had brought smoked fished, vobla, wrapped in Pravda. In return, although we hadn't talked about it, P had pulled out of his shopping bag a bottle of French wine which we drank toasting to peace and friendship between peoples. *You're completely lost, Comrade!* I am, like millions of people in this country where the red stars will soon cease to light the way. Who still believes in Communism? A few good souls in the heart of Russia, a few thousand Uzbeks to whom we brought electricity, irrigation and literacy, a few dozen Yakuts happy to read Lenin in their language, but who among Soviet elites, who in the Kremlin, who in the Yellow House still believes in the regime's continuity? *Vetrov, the prophet of doom.* Others before me, and more illustrious than me, considering the long list of persecuted scientists, artists, writers and simple folks, others have denounced the lie. Far from being a forerunner, I'll be the one giving the ultimate flick. Despair or hope, which will prevail?

What do you have to say about all this, little blatta orientalis? How blessed you are, you who existed under the Tsars, you who survived Lenin, Stalin, famine, war, purges, freeze, thaw, stagnation, you who will survive all powers for a long time, all utopian ideas and the resulting ideologies!

You want to find your place in history, Vetrov, as the one who sparked things off, the one who will have shaken the base of the Soviet superpower to its foundations, which it believed to be impregnable. No rational person will ever believe that you could achieve your dark deeds by passing on to amateurs some old dusty files forgotten at the bottom of a drawer. You'll do everything in your power to trivialize my actions, but you won't be able to deny them, truth always shines out. *What truth? The truth told by an alcoholic suffering from delirium tremens?!* No, the truth from a new kind of kamikaze, *you can scuttle yourself as you please, Vetrov,* my fall will cause the fall of the whole Empire, *a body collapsing in a courtyard will not stop the earth from going round.*

Vetrov the megalomaniac, a Russian trait, *you're just a mediocre player, you risk losing everything,* I must lose everything to be able to win everything, *you made a mistake by refusing to wash your dirty linen in public,* I did my absolute best to warn the authorities that the train wreck was unavoidable, *the Party is always right, Comrade,* that's what I had believed for a long time, then I started doubting and I began thinking on my own, judging, having personal opinions, critically assessing everything I was reading, hearing, and seeing. *And that's the way you became a dangerous deviationist.* The minute you start thinking independently, Comrade, there is nothing they can do against you. Try as they might, recalling me to Moscow, sending me to Siberia, locking me up in Lefortovo, they've not been able to prevent me from thinking! *You'll be less full of yourself in a few hours!* The fuse has been lit, *you're bluffing, Vetrov,* a time bomb is about to blow up, and all of you with it, they are just waiting for me to disappear before exploding it. *Is this some kind of bargaining?* I have nothing to hope for anymore, *are you so sure,* nothing left to expect from life, *what about spring in the shade of the Kresty willows,* life gave me everything, *you're the niggardly one, Vetrov,* I have my own way to give back to the Russian people what it offered me, whether you like it or not, I acted as a patriot, *a strange way to show your love for your country, Comrade!*

How could I have betrayed Russia to which I am attached with every fiber of my being, the little roach can testify to it. *I doubt its testimony would be taken into account.*

The ribbon of snow has melted. Winters are no longer what they used to be, imperious, brutal, cruel. A sneaky and slimy cold has surrounded the city and seeps through the walls. Chances are I will fall in mud with my arms spread. *Think about the shooting, Vetrov, think about the firing squad made up of young inexperienced recruits, imagine the bruised, torn, bloody flesh, imagine the bones blown to pieces, crushed, pulverized, above all reflect on the fact that it will be the first time those blue-eyed kids from middle Russia receive the command to load their gun, aim and fire. Think about what must go on in their consciences, Vetrov, no doubt they'll need several attempts to finish you off.*

I feel only contempt for your threats, your blackmail, your schemes. Those base police methods are stale. *Maybe so, but didn't you apply those methods yourself? And aren't you the one who clamors about his attachment to the Russian land? If you refuse to be exfiltrated, Vetrov, know that Mother Russia's coat is vast enough to shelter you. You keep out of the limelight for a few years, in Birobidzhan or in Kirghizia, your friends will think you're dead, then you reappear under a new identity! If you have the will, Vetrov, you have your whole life ahead of you.* As if it were possible to save one's skin, all we can hope is for the end to be delayed. *Dying in one's bed after a full life is what everyone aspires to, you don't have the right to fail your loved ones that way, Vetrov,* no, I don't have the right, my little fox, I don't have the right to leave you, Vladik and you, my sweetheart, frail and tender like birch bark, Svetik, my eternal spring!

And you, grandmother, are you going to abandon your intrepid little soldier? Are you going to forgive your Volodia's horrible sin? Aren't you the one, dearest grandmother, when the blizzard was raging outside, who opened my eyes on the Sirin bird and his rainbow plumage? And you, poor dad, poor mom, from where you are, can you understand how the sinner I am has come to reject their iniquitous laws and to submit to the Law of Love?

You won't even get a line in Pravda. A crime of passion, an ordinary murderer, an ordinary fellow in the grip of common passions who merely accomplished what fate had in store for him. *A loser who snapped; you shouldn't have come back to Moscow ever, Vetrov.* Had you been perceptive enough to foresee what was going to happen, you wouldn't have recalled Lieutenant Colonel Vladimir Ippolitovich Vetrov to the Center.

You are now alone, Vetrov, and you'll probably remain so forever. If relying only on appearances, I am indeed reduced to isolation, disowned by all; the solitude of the spy is terrible, *when he betrays the power he depends on; it was up to you not to sever the bond,* you can lock me up all you want, and force me to submission, you've not been able to prevent me from freeing myself. *We view as a disgrace what you call deliverance.* I'm not saying otherwise, I deserve to be convicted, I'm guilty of murder. *If that's all you were guilty of, you'd have been already pardoned by now!*

The little roach has become crazy, crawling on the wall, hiding under the bed or taking refuge at the bottom of the washbasin, pretending to disappear down the drain pipe, when I try to grab it. What is it trying to tell me? Is it a criticism of my wanting to play the hero? It's attached to me as much as I am to it. *Remember the blue roses.*

Blue like the Lada I was so attached to, as I am now attached to the cockroach. It was my faithful companion, *without it you could not have played the adventurer in the pocket park behind the Borodino Panorama Museum.*

How long I've been waiting in the blue Lada, freezing my butt, as the French say. There's nothing glamorous in the life of a spy, quite the contrary, it's a gray, tedious routine; characters change, *after Xavier, Marguerite came in*, a new character but the script was the same, *only this time around it was written by Vetrov, the illustrious illusionist.* Same place—*the pocket park*, and the Cheriomushki market—same day, on Fridays at eleven in the morning, *Friday is not a lucky day, Vetrov!* Christ died on a Friday, a thought I did not have in those days!

You should have thought about this Christ of yours whom you claim you found in the Gulag. He will help me go across this sea of blood, he will look over my loved ones, he will save Russia! *If you trust him that much, Vetrov, ask him to delay your execution by a couple of days, to the day after tomorrow, a Friday;* the day after tomorrow I will be forever in the blue Lada where, one after the other, Xavier, Marguerite, and Paul will come visit with me; *you're going crazy, Vetrov,* yes, I'm going crazy, running all over the place like you, little roach. *It's a tremendous emotional stress for a man alone, you need to refocus, Vetrov, that's what jail is for, and if you don't want others to censor, deform, shorten your story, it's for you to tell it to us without omissions. Before meeting Paul, who were you waiting for around ten thirty on the morning of May 8, 1981, at the Cheriomushki market?*

Time slowed down almost to a stop. In the crowd I saw Marguerite's peaceful face, I watched her as she bought cucumbers, potatoes, carrots, I watched her as she left the market exactly at eleven. I noticed the trembling of her eyelid when she spotted me. She hesitated to get in my car, I encouraged her, certain that no one had noticed us. She quickly hid in her shopping basket the file I handed her, and returned it the next day, Victory Day, in the pocket park. And so the ballet of rendezvous continued on the fifteenth, the sixteenth and the twenty-second of May, *you were playing with fire, Vetrov, I was taking risks, you went too far.* How fast Marguerite's heart must have been pounding when she found the shell fragment I had buried at the bottom of her basket! *That's not your only blunder, Vetrov, more will follow.* A calculated blunder, a signal to the French, a way to make them understand that I no longer accepted to deal with amateurs, however brave they were, *you had been dreaming of engineering your dark conspiracies with Paul since the evening under the cedar tree,* it was with him, and him alone, that I had decided to pull out all the stops. *You will then see your dear friend every Friday,* and every week, each Saturday in June, he spent the night making photocopies of hundreds of pages from top-secret documents, *until the day when he brought you a Minox,* a miniature camera allowing me to photograph everything that came through my office, *the leak of the century,* interrupted by Paul's summer vacation, *summer vacation is sacred for the French,* he could have raised suspicion by changing his schedule, *pretty casual about their mole, those French,* I needed rest too, *that's the least one can say, Vetrov, you felt you could not go on much longer playing your double game, you were close to having had enough, you started smoking American cigarettes again,* things were going poorly with Svetlana, *you didn't have many friends left,* I still had the dacha, the apple trees in Kresty, and the Tvertsa running carefree through the old willows. *Time flies by faster than you think, Vetrov, it would be your last summer in the countryside.*

Who is the spider, who is the fly? It's the biter bit ; I entered a turbulent zone, I was increasingly alone between two women, two countries, two worlds, *that's the fate of those who choose to betray,* you're confusing treason and transition, *when you leave one side of the river, you'd better be sure you'll make it to the other side,* I preferred to stop in the middle of the stream, *and you found yourself in the eye of the storm,* the impulse has been sent, the process has started, *but you're no longer in control, Vetrov, you're brooding on your vain deeds in a dark clink with a roach for a cellmate.*

I'm not explaining myself to you but to posterity, *oh, come off it, while you were fretting, that summer, your great friend didn't show much concern about you, he extended his stay in the French mountains,* he came back in September, tanned, thinner, *looking like the average Frenchman with his green parka and his corduroys,* I breathe again, the contact has been restored, *he is the one who made your schedule,* he was the only friend I had left during that time of my life, the only one I could share my torments with, *and you were naive enough Vetrov to pour out your feelings, Paul pretended to be interested in your qualms whereas the only thing of interest to him was the content of your shopping basket!*

I'm convinced that he is currently doing everything he can to get me out of here! *It's beyond his power, and you know it, Vetrov.* I willingly threw myself into the bear's jaws, I had to return to Moscow to gain access to sensitive information, I had to stay in Moscow to deliver the documents, and I could hand them out only to the French because I knew them well, and because I knew we did not take them seriously, which limited the risk of being caught red handed.

Your story is too beautiful, too smooth to be true, Vetrov. That summer, I was assailed with doubts and depression. Why deny it? And later, still, after Paul's return, I could not sleep at night. Would I be able to go all the way and complete this crazy self-assigned mission? *And if, smitten with legitimate remorse, you had started by bringing your shopping bag to headquarters, you could have come clean, pretending someone had tried to manipulate you, the military attaché would have been caught and expelled, twenty-four hours to pack, you would have been offered Prague or Budapest, Hungarian women have a certain something, and the paprika fish soup is delicious.* I never thought about doing such a volte-face. *It's never too late, Vetrov, think of the white shirt, remember stolen kisses on benches when the new leaves of the birch trees dance in the wind.*

Just yesterday, death was only an abstraction. Today, for the first time, I met Her in my cell, she's feeling at home here, she interferes between the roach and me. Shamelessly, she grabs the burgundy tie and knots it around her neck, she spreads her wings and invites me to ride on her back, claiming she will take me much farther away than the red rooster or the Sirin bird would do, she taps me on the shoulder and looks me up and down. *It will soon be your turn, Vetrov.* She's puffing herself up, she knows that she always wins in the end; now I recognize her, she is the cat in grandmother's folk tales, *the cat from Kazan who terrorizes mice*, pretending to grant me more time, blowing hot and cold, *they'll let you die like a rat, with your belly open, in horrible pain.*

So much suffering for nothing, Vetrov, you will have ended by being merely a tiny cog in the machine, and I'll be the last victim of the Soviet machine, *Vetrov quartered, crushed by the red wheel,* the instrument of fate, *a pathetic agent,* just like the violin in grandmother's tales, vanishing once the music has been played. *Your songs are grating, Vetrov, your violin is out of tune, you were drinking more and more during that Fall of 81, you were pouring out your heart, boasting to anyone who'd listen that you had influential friends who could provide you with a limo, a villa, and even cover you with medals.* They'll try to make me out to be a psychopath, I'll be accused of mental confusion, *and rightly so Vetrov, because of your incoherent ramblings, your close relations couldn't recognize you anymore.* They couldn't understand my transformation, conditioned by their Soviet education, they were unable to interpret the new Vetrov's behavior, *this new incarnation was scaring you too, you were just a trapped animal, Vetrov, you held it against the whole world, you talked too much, you told Vladik about your life, you wanted to flee with him, you claimed that Ludmila wanted to blackmail you. Vetrov, a man in dire straits.* How could it have been otherwise in my situation? *Even more so considering that your friend Paul was not around at all during that summer.* Over two months without seeing him, it was terribly difficult, but I never doubted him. *With each passing day, risks increased.* Yet I kept gathering information, I fine tuned the lists of our agents posted abroad, drew up the detailed profiles of the correspondents we had recruited, tallied everything we had stolen in various sectors, I put together a comprehensive nomenclature of our most sophisticated achievements in the military field, long evenings spent at the office, added to the work I was paid for. *No wonder they diagnosed a split in your personality!* Such dissociation affects every man and woman in this country forced to say the opposite of what they think.

You think you're a hero, Vetrov, I do, that year was the most thrilling in my life, *but your end will be sordid,* you'll have no trouble trashing my name, *you have blood on your hands,* History will do me justice, *the romance ended badly, Ludmila demanded that you leave Svetlana, she gave you an ultimatum of February twenty-two,* the day before my next rendezvous with Paul, *you were still trying to hedge your bets, Vetrov, you're a Libra, a tightrope walker, but your balancing act won't prevent you from tilting to the wrong side.*

You chose to see only the bad side of the story. How could you understand that my meetings with Paul in the pocket park were as vibrant as the most romantic trysts! *If the Lada could talk, it's not what it would recount, Vetrov, tell your admirers what happened in the evening of February 22, 1982, in your car parked in the empty lot, tell your female fans how, after drinking champagne to celebrate with Ludmila, you used the empty bottle to hit her on the head; she was struggling, you grabbed the meat hook and planted it in her mouth, tell us about her teeth knocked off, the screaming of terror-stricken Ludmila, the thrusting of the hook into her flesh, the blood spurting out onto the seats, your clothes, explain to us how you had to make several attempts—the bitch didn't want to die, Ludmila is a healthy woman, she resists—she manages to open the door, you want to pursue her but an unexpected witness shows up, you totally lose it, hit in the heart, the retired policeman collapses. Ludmila, bleeding to death, crawls all the way to the bus stop where a good soul calls an ambulance, Ludmila is rushed to the hospital but not before she had the time to describe you and the Lada.*

Little roach, you're the only one who doesn't judge me, the only one who doesn't fear the murderer, the only one who finds extenuating circumstances to his case. *You forget Vladik and Svetlana.* Moscow is not a friendly city for lovers, nowhere to find a cozy nest. *It's not Moscow's fault, Vetrov.* According to

Ludmila, some of my colleagues knew that I was meeting with some Frenchmen. She was willing to tell them everything if I didn't leave Svetlana. I panicked. *This is no justification for the murder and the murder attempt.* It was the next day that P was supposed to exfiltrate me by hiding me in the trunk of his car, Ludmila's ultimatum jeopardized the plan. *And what if you had decided to commit your crime in cold blood? As a way out of the trap you had got yourself into! Your ruse almost worked, Vetrov. And the Service was ready to believe you, fearing leaks about this affair. The psychologist would have certified mental disorder, you would have been declared unfit for the Service and dismissed, you would have received a light sentence for form's sake, you would have found the right tree to hide the forest of your crimes against the Soviet State's security!*

On February 23, *almost three years ago, Vetrov,* I was arrested. On the 24th, Svetlana had to return my Party card and my decorations to the authorities. My trial in camera went on for seven months, *long enough to fill the seven thick gray-bound volumes,* in September I was sentenced to fifteen years' imprisonment. *Your legs started trembling when you heard the verdict, blood left your face, you looked like a ghost.* Svetlana paid for the policeman's funeral and paid Ludmila compensation. *What about your French friends, where were they and what were they doing?*

Nothing can justify my criminal act, *you're a mere bedbug to be stepped on, a petty trafficker, a careerist, an insignificant murderer who attempted to get rid of his mistress in a parking lot,* the steamroller is on its way, you've isolated me completely before eliminating me, *we were ready to play down the affair,* you'll keep discrediting me, *Ludmila did not talk, Vetrov,* you'll hold me up to public obloquy, it was snowing that evening but snow cannot erase everything, you'll fabricate evidence, *Vladik had only one thing on his mind, washing the car, washing away his father's crime,* you'll make up conspiracy stories, *Svetlana did not betray you,* my little fox, my love, my darling, take care of yourself, I know you forgave me, but you Ludmila, sweetheart, how could you forget this horror, this killing frenzy, *you don't deserve your women, Vetrov,* they'll all be quick to defile my miserable end; you'll try to reduce my destiny to that sordidness, *you can count on us to do everything in our power so that Vetrov's name will be dishonored forever,* this is the fate reserved for those who demand to stand out.

Forget the black Peugeot, Vetrov, forget the blue Lada, forget your pseudo friends, you appealed to them for help, Jacques I'm asking you to help my family, *they turned a deaf ear, they no longer need you; it's not our way to look at it, Vetrov, you can redeem yourself, you can still be useful, since you're so fond of cars, why not get into the one still parked in front of the Praga?* A last chance, a new adventure, a new life, could it be?

Your worst enemy, Vetrov, it's not us, it's yourself! Where was I? The threads are entangled, the recent past is pushing back the older past. *We can help you reconstruct your biography.* Where did I stop? The present is swaying under my feet, I lose my way, I go down dead-end roads, I backtrack, *you're looking for a future for yourself, Vetrov, it can be arranged, our experts know as much as Paul on the lizard's tactics, how many missing persons thought to be dead reappeared years, even decades later!* But why would you grant me such an opportunity and how could I still be useful? Didn't I tell you my whole story a hundred times? *We are gold diggers, Vetrov, it's by panning the sand in the river over and over that one eventually discovers the nugget.*

Why harass me this way? What do I need to confess that you don't already know? God, why did you abandon me, and you my friends, where are you? I feel my life crumbling, I become confused with the chronology, I can't remember how long I was in jail, then in the penitentiary camp, then in jail again, essential links vanish, and whereas I am overwhelmed with trivial details, you stole my time, you seized it, *we merely recovered it,* all this questioning eventually got the better of me, I fear I may slide into my own abysses, a fatal slide down a wall with nothing to hold on to.

Don't worry, Vetrov, our experts have written it all down, hour by hour, minute by minute and, if need be, they'll know how to reshape your story which is no longer yours. After six months in jail, in March, 1983, the judicial authorities decided to have you transferred to the penitentiary #272/3, a camp located not far from Irkutsk. A stay in Siberia, Vetrov, that's the least we could do for you. Thank the Party, thank the Soviet people, they will have made it possible for you to travel, first to the West, in France and North America, the day will come when any Russian citizen will be able to go there freely, the day is near when you are forced to open the borders, and then to the East at the workers' expense, the workers of our illustrious motherland. You'll have seen it all, Vetrov, both sides of the coin.

Rasputitsa. This word accurately refers to this dissipation of oneself, this decay of the being. Rasputitsa when roads become impassable, and vehicles get stuck in muddy tracks. Spring rasputitsa resulting from the thaw, and fall rasputitsa resulting from the rains. My stay in the penitentiary took place between the first and the second one. The time of debacle has come, I'll no longer pull out all the stops, I am alone, helpless, wading through a fuzzy world, I won't see the end of the monster. How could I open the doors to the future if I am not capable of pulling myself together!

Yet, you hung on, Vetrov, you started to believe in your lucky star again, you were constantly writing to Svetlana. I had the feeling that I would go home soon. Illusion? What I know for a fact is that I would not have become what I am today, twenty-third of January nineteen-eighty-five, without this dive into the Siberian cauldron which has always amalgamated Russian aristocrats, Decembrists, anarchists, Polish Catholics, Ukrainian and Baltic patriots, sincere communists, Korean and German prisoners, insurgents from Central Asia and rebels from the Caucasus, dissidents from all walks of life; I wouldn't have become who I am if I hadn't met so many cheerful fellows and rebellious characters there, offenders, traffickers, con men with whom you soon found common ground, Vetrov. You made yourself helpful, they liked you, you were exempted from chores, you were promised a job as a warehouseman. Wherever you go you make friends, tell us about your buddies in misfortune, Vetrov, tell us about Siberia!

"My grandfather and my father died in the Gulag," Lev had told me. An animal warmth radiated from the zek's body. I'll never forget the moment when we exchanged glances for the first time, this faint transparency lighting the camp night. He was a poet, Lev, he could make us cry in the evening, in the barracks. He would improvise threnodies celebrating the millions of martyrs sacrificed to build dams, canals, railroad tracks, the millions of slaves condemned to mine gold, lead, uranium, the thousands of squalid barracks where the outcasts excluded from the workers' paradise were rotting. "Time to sleep," shouted the warder, a woman. How could one go to sleep hearing the police dogs bark, seeing the sentries on the watch towers turn their searchlights on the prisoner who tried to escape. Lev feared nothing and no one. Every now and then, standing on his pallet, he raised a vengeful fist and shouted at his torturers. He had been transferred from camp to camp, they had inflicted every possible vexation on him, no one succeeded in silencing him. The vast plains of Siberia and the gigantic rivers were his allies, and so was the East wind which he called for rescue every night.

The East wind rises, murmurs, moans, hammers, howls, insults, it comes from afar, from Magadan, from the Kolyma, one gust after another, bolting horses with bloodshot eyes, accusing fingers, millions of dead rising from their anonymous graves, millions of zeks with their shaven heads, enemies of the people, left-wing deviationists, right-wing opportunists, mad dogs, foul-smelling creatures, lackeys of capitalism, Hitlero-Trotskyists, bourgeois nationalists, Zionists, Titoists, Bukharinists, fascist spies, hooligans, Poles, Tatars, decadents, Baltic traitors, quislings, political carrions, why the denunciations, why the arrests, why this obsession with purges, why eavesdropping everywhere, show trials, forced confessions? The howling wind sweeps through the country, is about to surround the Kremlin, to rush down the corridors and sneak under the General Secretary's door. Soon it won't be possible to suppress the innocents' complaint any longer.

He tends to get hysterical, your Lev, a criminal who killed a communist! It was a crime of passion, the communist tried to take his girlfriend away from him during a dance, Lev lost his temper, the fight turned out badly. *A drunkard, your friend, a vagrant, a guy who lost his bearings, birds of a feather flock together.*

We were in the same work unit, I never grew tired of listening to my friend Lev, my roommate who taught me how to warm to cockroaches.

"Under the Russian," said Lev, "the Asian shows, look at my cheekbones, look at my eyes." Russia with two faces. Unsettled country. The Russian capers about between Heaven and Earth. Russian mirages, old demons that never died. Could it be that Russia deserves only the yoke and the knout? Could it be that the Russian people made a pact with sorrow? They'll never stop seeking shelter under the Virgin's blue mantle.

A trove of stories, Lev: dead people coming back as frogs on the shores of Lake Kitai, a forest spirit welcoming lost travelers in his izba sculpted in the clouds, and the Kingdom of the White Waters one can reach only by dying seven times. Listening to Lev, I had the impression of living each of my seven lives again, going back to this long ago summer, in the village by the Volga, where I learned about the Kingdom of the White Waters for the first time from my grandmother's lips.

Nomadic Russia, muddy trails, lost villages, no one knows where it all begins and where it all ends. Lev wanted to take me to the North and show me a Christ sitting in the center of a fresco painted by a peasant. First, he wanted me to meet his friend the shaman, encountered in Yakutia. The shaman sees through darkness, *may he light the way for you, Vetrov*, he is the artisan of rebirth, he is the one who plants the birch tree at the center of the yurt, the tree of the three worlds uniting the fire, the earth and the heavens. The black and white tree that reconciles here and now, the past and the future.

You're rambling, Vetrov, you're talking nonsense, you're lapsing into obscurantism, it's due to my name, *Vetrov, the producer of hot air, fond of twaddle, hollow ideas form at the tip of your straw like soap bubbles! Grandmother from Simbirsk must have told you about the "airy-fairy woolly thoughts" of the peasant on his way to town to sell eggs at the market. Before selling them, he already dreams of what he'll do with the money. He'll buy chicks, and when they become chickens, he'll sell them to buy a sow which will give birth to piglets; by selling them he'll be able to own a cow which is bound to calve; he'll trade the calf for a horse, and finally, it goes without saying that a peasant who owns a horse will have a house built and will become a master. Just when the peasant could imagine his dearest dreams come true, the cart hit a stone, the basket fell over, breaking the eggs, and our muzhik found himself back where he started! You aimed too high, Vetrov, your basket is empty, all you have left is the white shirt and the paper roses.*

Even after I'm gone, my life will live on for others, I no longer try to control time but let it flow. "If you let yourself be grabbed by Siberia," Lev told me, "it will swallow you up, you'll rot there, but if you come to terms with it, you'll be reborn, crisp as a snowdrop. Everlasting spring is within reach, Vetrov, open your eyes and contemplate, the river is blue, the taiga is green and Siberia, the place of all new beginnings, is turned toward the future."

Siberia turned you into a poet, Vetrov, you the talker, here you took up writing, flooding your family with letters. The food is bad, we go hungry, my companions and I, we spend long days in the taiga cutting wood, there is nothing else to do here apart from standing twenty-five to forty minutes in the rain during inmate roll call, enough to get a bad cold, you're soaked, there is no place to dry your clothes, but you're not allowed to complain. Getting sick in this forlorn place is a calamity, you are given the same medicine for all illnesses, just like in Lefortovo. *Yet, penitentiary #272/3 has a good reputation, Vetrov.* True, it is thought to be a kindergarten compared to Magadan, the Kolyma or other camps! *That's when you began to understand the joys and attraction of freedom. You recalled Maxim's, La Tour d'Argent,* I thought about the pink villa, *you remembered the Saturday afternoons spent shopping at Tati's,* there hasn't been a single night when I didn't see Svetlana's red suit in my sleep. *Your first Sunday in Paris, Svetlana, all smiles, and you, you drove up the Champs-Elysées.*

I want so much to take you in my arms, Svetik, how I would like to kneel in front of you, to kiss your lips, life goes on, we must keep fighting, the fire is raging, I'm afraid it will spread, become all-consuming, but I fear no disaster. I am Russian, dorogaya, but I know they'll deny me the right to belong to this country, I'm not a monster, even if I killed, there are many ways to love, I'll never be able to return all that you gave me, those thousand of tasty dishes you cooked for me and which I was crazy about, especially when we were abroad, do you remember this beetroot borsch on a winter night in Montreal, and all the kindnesses you lavished on me, *the carefully chosen tie*, the shirt you ironed lovingly although you suspected I was having an affair, I miss your body, your skin so soft, so white, my little woman, do you know that every day as the evening draws near, I slip away into the forest to think about you, I hug a young birch tree asking for your forgiveness, biryoza moya, my little birch, you didn't forget the loving names we exchanged, for me you'll always be the beautiful bride ready to soar on Lenin Hills!

As death is approaching you're growing wings, Vetrov, come back to earth, your season is winter, you can't live without Moscow grayness, you need pacing up and down its muddy streets, you like underhand tricks, you're fond of rendezvous in isolated corners, you're the man who attempted to kill Ludmila and, whatever you do, you won't be able to forget the blood that doesn't want to dry on the Lada bench seat. I went mad, madly in love, my sweetheart, you became afraid, you thought I was getting away from you, you did everything you could to keep me, *she did everything to bring you back to the straight and narrow, all the women bend over backwards to save comrade Vetrov.* I thought I could hedge my bets, keeping Svetlana and Vladik, whom I adore, and you, Ludmila, whom I loved, and above all earning the respect of my Russian motherland which I wanted free, all those bonds were painful, each of these loves wanted exclusivity, *you're making progress, Vetrov, it is about time that you see yourself for what you are.* One must die seven times to reach the Kingdom of the White Waters.

It's snowing in Moscow. The snow falls more and more heavily, a nasty wind plasters the snowflakes against the window. Impossible to tell if the snow swirls are ascending or descending. What are you doing, Lev, where are you? Do you think that the snow violin will no longer play its music? The story of this violin born from the snowstorm and showing me the way, in which childhood had I heard it? God save us from another impostor who might want to appropriate the instrument to replay the discordant tunes we've known too well!

Whimsical, ephemeral snow, nothing lasts forever in life, tears dry, sorrow eases, and for what we can't forget, at least we see it differently. *You're not overburdened by remorse, Vetrov, you didn't learn a thing in the penitentiary camp.* I never cherished life more than when I was there, I never experienced brotherhood so intensely, I never looked at the earth, the trees, the clouds, the sky with so much love, I never cried so much, and above all I never laughed as much as I did in Siberia. *We should put you in charge of writing praise of the Gulag, Vetrov.*

Lev played a big part in this art of converting tragedy into comedy. *The scoundrel understood your true nature, he saw in you the chameleon, the one-man band able to play all the parts, Vetrov, the man with multiple boxes, the Soviet box, the French cash-register box, the family box, the Ludmila box and more.*

It is true that after undergoing all of this questioning and cross-examinations, after all those endlessly rehashed accusations you contrived to attach to me, I grew tired and gave up seeing myself the way I am, to see myself the way you see me, a dull, potbellied and libidinous nobody; without trying, you freed me from myself, and that's when I started laughing at all the characters you paraded in front of me like so many puppets to shoot down, the womanizer, the brilliant conversationalist, the false friend, the cuckold, the whole story ended up looking laughable to me, the secret documents among cucumbers and carrots, Paul with a backache from leaning over the copy machine; the more I remembered the unfolding of this affair, the more I viewed my life as interwoven between sequences having no apparent logical link, and the more I had the feeling of being infinitely fragmented.

One Vetrov gives way to another, you're nobody, Vetrov, I assumed all the parts, *you've lived just to become a melodrama actor, a pathetic character from a violent thriller,* that's the way you present me in your endless reports, your tedious court records, *there is no shortage of qualifiers to describe you*, false accusations must have been easy to obtain, *Vetrov the careerist, debauched, vengeful, ungrateful, frustrated, conceited, jealous, adventurer, wheeler-dealer, compulsive liar, and the list goes on;* "unto those that have shall more be given," I grant you that, I recognize myself in all these terms, you've examined me from every angle, the Vetrov case in seven grayish volumes where everything, absolutely everything, is recorded but the essential. And you're not that stupid that you don't know it. Why set yourselves against me so relentlessly if I was merely a mediocre actor, a anti-hero?

No one will view you as a hero, Vetrov. If you're so sure, why all this agitation? Do you believe I am so naive that I cannot imagine what you're going to invent about me? Certainly the time of the Moscow show trials is no more. It would be risky to attempt to humiliate me in front of cameras from all over the world. No more thundering litany intended to pillory the class enemy and brand him as fascist. *That would be giving you too much credit!* You already told me, all I deserve is a line in the paper. *Claiming to be the wrecker of the great Soviet dream is ludicrous, Vetrov, you're just a red-nosed clown, a remnant of the Cold War, a wreck.*

You refuse to see the other Vetrov, too alarming for you, as he will be seen by future generations, the anti-hero hero at the juncture of two worlds and two eras. *It's your nature to blow hot air, you'd be better off giving some thought about a way to save your hide, otherwise you'll soon be reduced to a corpse shoved into a bag, and nobody will know where you're buried.* Even if you scatter my ashes to the four cardinal points, Vetrov will slip through your fingers, before long the old world will collapse, soon there will be only renegades in this land.

You won't be such a braggart when the two henchmen grab you under the arms, and the third one points his weapon at you! And if he needs several attempts, that will give you time to replay the film of your fall. What memories will I take with me into the tunnel, will it be Paul's irony, the little red suit or Vladik's peaceful voice? Or will it be the evenings in Kresty, the dinners in Paris, the pink sky over the taiga? The darkness surrounding me will tear open and all of a sudden immense fireworks will appear to me. *Did you correctly consider the consequences of your actions? However twisted and warped, it is the communist idea which willy-nilly kept together and united millions of people outside as well as inside the bloc.* And it was against this idea, and against its travesty, that more millions of human beings rose up.

The uncontrollable Vetrov will have been motivated by only one goal, the dissolution of the Soviet empire. And he accomplished his task methodically, spending countless nights at the office to photograph tons of documents, the three thousand pages of top-secret archives, a list of over four hundred Soviet agents posted abroad, the plan to occupy France if attacked, the proof that the Soviet Union had succeeded in obtaining in the West thirty thousand devices and over four hundred thousand documents making it possible to copy missiles, space shuttles, navigation and radar protection systems. Moreover, agent Farewell transmitted the code names of all the sophisticated Soviet programs, along with the research plan for the Academy of Science and his country's laboratories, all of this wrapped in newspaper pages from Pravda and shoved into the housewife's shopping basket or in a plastic bag thrown onto the backseat of the blue Lada!

1983. The darkest year for our Service since its inception. But chances are you will no longer be around to witness the results of your harmful deeds, Vetrov. If your French friends, overeager to get back into favor with their American ally, hadn't expelled the forty-seven Soviet diplomats in April, referring to a secret document you were among the very few to know, and producing it as evidence, we wouldn't have known, Vetrov, that you were the mole! How could you trust people who cared so little about your safety? Not a single postcard from Jacques or Paul, not the slightest decoration, not even a thank you from President Mitterrand who went to Washington to bow before Reagan and present him with your revelations in order to be forgiven for having appointed four communist ministers to his administration. You chose the wrong side, Vetrov, you let them dazzle you in Paris, they cast a spell on you in the park of the pink villa. You will make a convenient scapegoat, Vetrov, once you're dead, they'll put whatever words they want into your mouth. All their murky deals, their Taiwan frigates, their Swiss bank accounts, the illegal wire tapping by the Elysée, it will all be your fault, and when your friends no longer need you, they'll conspire in your non-existence. Farewell? A set up by the Americans! Volodia? A decoy invented by both sides. And once the decoy has done the job, he is discarded and falls into oblivion!

It stopped snowing. It's warmer again. Moscow is immerged in slush. Official cars speed through pools of water, splashing the pedestrians. The roach curled up in my palm, staying with me.

There is an infinite number of Vetrovian masks, but there is only one Vetrov, the one who sensed the outcome, the one who sees the colossus shaking on its bases, the one heralding a major upheaval. There will be more jolts and convulsions before the dinosaur draws its last breath and before Russia resolves to renounce its imperial dream, just as the other European nations did. Despite denying it, Russia at her beginning partook of the same spirit that gave birth to Europe, and if Europe needs Russia, Russia needs Europe even more.

Anything can happen, Vetrov, warmer East-West relations, a new political order, it shouldn't be long coming, your destiny is in your hands, I am only the instrument of my fate, *everything is still possible, a posting in the Caribbean Islands, a pension paid by the French,* I would more easily picture myself painting icons in a monastery, *Vetrov, our Vetrov at Saint-Georges, that's an idea, we're open to all viewpoints, think it over, time is short, if you want to live.* I want to live, but the form in which I'll survive is of little concern to me, *in the flesh, Vetrov, that's in that form and state Svetlana and Vladik want you back!* They say the dead keep on thinking, loving, suffering, *this is not Marxist thinking, Vetrov,* it's a thought from Lev, a dream from grandmother, a noble idea from the times of blue icons. *Do you truly expect recognition after you're gone, Vetrov? Think about the white shirt!*

Jacques had invited us to a Piaf concert at the Paris Olympia. Parisians turned round as you went by, my lovely poppy, but you only had eyes for me, dashing in my navy blue suit. It was on this occasion that I wore for the first time the white shirt from Lanvin and the burgundy tie. You had wanted to walk up the Champs-Elysées on my arm. 'Non, rien de rien...' you were humming Piaf's song while showering me with adoring glances. How I loved you! *How you loved Paris, Vetrov, and France which made a lasting impression on you.* 'Non, rien de rien, non, je ne regrette rien,' no, I'm not sorry for anything. He that is without sin among you, let him first cast a stone at me!

That was a long time ago, Vetrov, a very long time ago; last month, just before New year's Eve, Svetlana was able to pass a letter to Jacques asking for his help, but your French friends did not bother to answer, too busy savoring their fines de claire oysters and sipping their champagne without you.

I hear you but what you're saying no longer concerns me. Vetrov is already elsewhere, neither in Paris nor in Moscow, he is no longer in the here and now, he is reaching the other side. Life has taught him that a human being isn't just his role in society, that he can't be reduced to the list of his deeds, good and bad. Man is larger than man, he defies definition. Yes, the darkness surrounding us is about to tear open, *you're not about to see the light again, Vetrov,* and soon millions of East and West Europeans will be able to meet as they please. Seeing Paris will no longer be an impossible dream. A Soviet man will be allowed to fall in love with a French woman without being suspected of collusion with the enemy.

Change of plan, Vetrov, we just received new instructions, the car has left the Praga and is now waiting in front of the prison. An amicable settlement acceptable to all parties is possible. The French are not as ungrateful as we had thought. They are ready to get you out of the hole. You have one hour, we are determined to look the other way and let your friends believe they can carry it off. The bird Vetrov flies away, we announce your death, you keep a low profile for a while, then we make contact with you again for a new mission. There is a new life ahead, Vetrov.

I am through with the endless war of shadows in which one no longer knows who he is and who the other is. *Only the one with control over all his masks can save his skin.* It's ages since I stopped worrying about my skin, I wanted to give a meaning to my life, different from the one you wanted to impose. *The only meaning your life had was to serve the Soviet motherland.* According to you, the only way out is to consent to being confined in time the way you define it. *No human being escapes this confinement.* And what if it were possible to project oneself beyond the time limits allotted to each of us?

Who am I? Who am I before I'm born? Who am I after I'm dead? Those are the questions confronting me today. And the escape I am hoping for is not the one you're offering me. If I returned to this country you condemned to silence, it's not to prolong my life to no avail. *Useless blathering, you'll return to the Russian land which will swallow you up like an ordinary cockroach!* Ashes to ashes, dust to dust, this doesn't bother me, this is the common lot; what drives me is reaching the passage, going through the metamorphosis requiring that I become who I am. Death is nothing but a new beginning, it is the moment when the old and the new Vetrov become one. For Vetrov to live on, he must be shot. And the bullet hitting my heart will be the signal for the big collapse.

The car just drove away, without you, be ready to die alone, Vetrov, this is my ultimate trial, crossing the sea of blood. *You're lucky, Vetrov, it is snowing again and the firing squad is waiting for you in the courtyard.* Grinding of keys in the locks, and again the scratching of the scrubbing brush, *just the time to put the white shirt on,* and already the noise of the rifle butts, *the last time you knot the burgundy tie,* and the snapping sound of weapons being loaded, *goodbye Farewell,* farewell warder and you, the old hag, farewell blue roses, farewell my beloved, I won't die alone, the little roach is clinging to the tie, I imagine my body falling in the fresh snow in a few minutes, the corpse picked up and shoved into a bag before being thrown into the common grave. I imagine the shape drawn by my body, with my arms spread in the melting snow. I fear nothing now. As if this gesture were a logical conclusion, I raise my arms without clutching my fists and with my index and major fingers making the v of 'veter', the wind in the wings of Victory rising above the Wall and beyond the gloomy horizon of the prison of nations, the subtle smile of the poet appears on my lips at the very moment when the young soldiers point their rifles at me. And I see, as the command to fire resounds, the cockroach spread its rainbow wings and fly away, and as the bullets shatter my bones and the blood spurts out on the shirt I hear the exquisite music of the snow violin.

Epilogue

This haunting and agonizing inner dialogue is a fiction. Who could pretend to reconstruct with certainty the chaotic thoughts and the rehashed memories that beset a man during the few hours preceding his execution? Here, I did not intend to be a biographer. This narrative is meant to be an immersion into the consciousness of the character facing himself and looking back on his life in order to discern its meaning.

If, after much thought, I felt authorized to substitute myself for Vladimir Ippolitovich at this critical time in his life, it is on several accounts that I want to explain. However I would like to emphasize that this book could not have been written had I judged the condemned man or not felt a profound empathy with him.

On January 23, 1985, the day Vladimir Vetrov was executed, I was in Moscow, posted at the French embassy where I officiated as Cultural Attaché in charge of artistic exchanges. I was offered this position because as early as 1967 I had chosen to live in Eastern Europe in order to establish cultural relations with the peoples of those countries, anxious to free themselves from the yoke of Communism. I had fulfilled a first mission in Moscow in the mid-seventies. When I left my teaching job in June, 1975, I knew nothing of Vladimir Ippolitovich Vetrov's existence, I did not know he had returned, in March of the same year, from Montreal to his native town, and I did not suspect that I myself would be back eight years later in the Soviet capital.

Above all, without me knowing it at the time, there was a link between my second assignment, in the fall of 1983, and the huge intelligence leak orchestrated by Vetrov. It is indeed thanks to the lists provided by Farewell that Mitterrand gave the green light for the expulsion from France, in the spring of that same year, of forty-seven diplomats proven guilty of espionage. Relations were strained between the two countries, on the verge of breaking off. It is no surprise, in such a context, that I had to wait several weeks for authorization from Soviet authorities. The delivery of my entry visa in October, 1983, was viewed by the French side as the litmus test of a relative warming in the relations between the two countries.

This period was one of the most exciting in my professional life. Over just a few years, General Secretaries of the Communist Party of the Soviet Union would follow one another, Brezhnev, Andropov, Chernenko, Gorbachev: the political line was uncertain, a hardening remained a possibility. Openness without laxness, prudence without rigidity, two irons in the fire, this pragmatic approach was the best suited for those transition times between stagnation and perestroika. A subtle game that was reviewed day by day in order to strike a balance, fueling tough debates within our very embassy. While I was actively promoting exchanges in my sphere of responsibilities, finding great satisfaction in making things change, I would also get quite disheartened at times. The self-perpetuating empire of stagnation preserved its vices. Repression continued, and I myself was not spared threats, punctured tires, phone calls in the middle of the night, and other intimidation tactics. Several members of our embassy were expelled; the surveillance became tighter around the French community. One of the forty-seven spies became Head of International Relations for the Ministry of Culture, and was therefore my inevitable interlocutor. 1984, as heralded by Orwell, was truly a decisive year.

For the foreigners who lived there, there is a before Russia and an after Russia. I would take away with me from that country an entrenched abhorrence of totalitarianism and an acute awareness that this scourge could plague any nation. It is also in Eastern Europe, however, that I became certain that human beings, whether standing up or pretending to bow, could resist tyranny. Thus it became a natural thing for me to join the dissidence and learn how to fight the subversive activities of a system that claimed to eventually reign over the whole world. My anti-communist feelings, resulting from my experience on the ground, were the exact counterpart of the anti-Nazi feelings of my father whom I admired. The analogy between the two systems was obvious to me. And so the Cultural Attaché I was became a shadow fighter, after being recruited by P, who was Vetrov's handling officer. Fortunately, I did not have to live through the trials and tribulations of a double agent. My minuscule activity in this domain cannot be compared with Vetrov's colossal achievement. I am proud of having provided my superiors, as early as the end of 1984, with information coming from the Kremlin's physician who predicted the upheaval perestroika would turn out to be. And I would later be informed by one of the forty-seven expelled diplomats about the likely rise of Boris Yeltsin to the supreme position. Above all, I experienced the agent's solitude from within, sufficient to be able to imagine what Vladimir Vetrov went through, having to face obstacles much more formidable than those I encountered. "The French," P had confided when I was leaving on assignment, "only appreciate the gendarme and the soldier when they feel under threat. As for the spy and the counterspy, they like them only in the movies. Our elites are primarily concerned about not dirtying their hands. In France one doesn't dine with a spy, they're only to be mocked for their blunders. In other climes, the shadow fighter, who protects his country's military, scientific and industrial secrets, enjoys the general public's respect. He may even be assigned important duties. In France, choosing to be a spy will make you lose your reputation if not your life. Moreover, fighting against Communism has never been popular in our country, where being an anti-communist has been equated for half a century to being a fascist. The French were last in the West to grasp what Soviet totalitarianism meant."

Some time after the collapse of the Berlin Wall, I met P again, and we talked about Farewell. "I stood back," he said then, "I'm savoring time going by while trying to understand the ins and outs of this affair, something the agent out in the field doesn't necessarily perceive. In the seventies, Andropov, who was then the KGB Chairman, had become convinced that the regime was doomed. It was then he conceived the project of purging the Party and ousting Brezhnev and his clan. The underhanded struggle that followed between the proponents of the status quo and the supporters of change reached a critical point at the time when relations with the United States were especially tense. There was such a climate of paranoia on both sides that the dreaded nuclear conflict seemed more and more possible. It is precisely at that moment that Vladimir Vetrov intervened, admirably positioned to accurately appreciate the risks for the planet and the threats to peace. It is thus with full knowledge of the facts that Vetrov, alone, decided to destabilize the system in order to avert a disastrous confrontation and force his country to reform. For the Soviet power, the Farewell affair was not just an astonishing leak of information, it was a flood, a tidal wave, a true disaster!"

During our conversation, I carefully avoided asking P why Mitterrand, after using the gift from Farewell to come back into the White House's favor, pretended to believe that the French counterintelligence's achievement was a disinformation operation led by the Americans to hamper the French-Soviet rapprochement. American provocation or Soviet intrigue? Such assumptions are groundless. They were voiced only to cover up political maneuvers ongoing in France at the time. "They have tried to discredit Farewell, but the future will do him justice," simply said P, without complaining about having been unfairly dismissed despite the dominant role he played, along with his spouse, and Jacques and Xavier, in the biggest success achieved by French counterespionage in the twentieth century.

"There is a before Farewell and an after Farewell," wrote Raymond Nart, the brilliant head of French counterespionage at the Directorate of Territorial Surveillance, the DST. It cannot be emphasized enough that Vladimir Vetrov should not be reduced to his ambitions, his torments, his loves, his hatreds, his weaknesses, his crime, his treason. He was also, and above all, an agent with nerves of steel, carrying on his solitary fight and bringing to completion the grand project he had conceived. Treason was the only way for him to break the deadlock that had been poisoning international relations for several decades. "Hero or traitor?" wonders journalist Sergei Kostin in his detailed analysis devoted to Vladimir Vetrov. Anti-hero, but also hero of our time, Vetrov stood at the cusp of two eras. He was a forerunner whose complex and peculiar destiny foreshadowed the dismantlement of the camp he belonged to. It was necessary for Vetrov, somehow mirroring the fate of his country, to transform himself from torturer into victim. He had to go down with his ship and die for History to enter a new phase. Whatever the seriousness of his sins, Vladimir Ippolitovich Vetrov answered to the call and did not hesitate to leap from secret to mystery, thus giving full meaning to his passage on this earth in the twentieth century. "Volodia," said P, "was an ordinary, life-loving Russian. It took an immense courage for him to accomplish the mission he assigned himself; he is the one who changed the course of the world." In answer, I told P that "I had come to realize that for you those swaps of grocery bags at the market were more beautiful than a romance, and I know that if you had the faintest hope of seeing Farewell alive again, you'd walk across Russia to find him."

Christmas 2007